MURDER ON THE FRONTIER

MURDER ON THE FRONTIER

ERNEST HAYCOX

Thorndike Press • Chivers Press
Thorndike, Maine USA   Bath, Avon, England

DM JH RK

This Large Print edition is published by Thorndike Press, USA and by Chivers Press, England.

Published in 1996 in the U.S. by arrangement with Golden West Literary Agency.

Published in 1996 in the U.K. by arrangement with Golden West Literary Agency.

U.S. Hardcover 0-7862-0653-5 (Western Series Edition)
U.K. Hardcover 0-7451-4752-6 (Chivers Large Print)
U.K. Softcover 0-7451-4753-4 (Camden Large Print)

Copyright © 1931, 1933, 1934, 1936, 1937, 1942 by the Crowell Collier Corporation. Copyright renewed 1959, 1961, 1962, 1964, 1965, 1970, by Jill Marie Haycox.

These stories appeared in *Collier's* magazine from June, 1931 to February, 1942.

First published in book form by Little, Brown and Company in 1952.

All rights reserved.

Thorndike Large Print ® Western Series.

The text of this Large Print edition is unabridged.
Other aspects of the book may vary from the original edition.

Set in 16 pt. News Plantin by Minnie B. Raven.

Printed in the United States on permanent paper.

British Library Cataloguing in Publication Data available

Library of Congress Catalog Card Number: 95-91002
ISBN 0-7862-0653-5 (lg. print : hc)

CONTENTS

CONTENTS

McQuestion Rides

When Matt McQuestion came through the throat of the low pass and paused to regard the ranch below he already had made a thorough and unobserved survey of the roundabout hills; and there was in him a rising belief that the man he wanted — a legal John Doe whose face he never had seen — was at present sheltered down there.

Proceeding down the slope, Matt McQuestion observed all things with the senses of an old hunter. A sodden, cloud-congested sky lent an uneasy dimness to the day, and the wind ripped wildly against higher trees to create the fury of some vast cataract pouring into a chasm. Faintly through this sounded the beating of the ranch triangle, announcing noon; a pair of riders cantered homeward from an opposite slope. House and outbuildings seemed to crouch beneath the tempest and in a distant hillside corral a bunch of horses stood passively dejected, backs humped and tails driven between their legs. As McQuestion drew beside the house porch a stout and florid man emerged.

7

"Light an' come in," he bellowed. "Judas, what a day to fare forth! Lonny — come, take this horse to the barn!

But the rider kept his place until he had observed the necessary amenities. "My name," said he, "is Matt McQuestion, sheriff of the county."

"Heard of you and mighty pleased to have you drum your knuckles against my door!" shouted the ranchman. "I'm French Broadrick! You're just in time to eat! Get down, sir, get down! We're too condemned polite for good health! Lonny, take the horse!"

McQuestion dismounted then, surrendered his pony to an appearing puncher and, at Broadrick's continued gesture, moved inside. Crossing to the bright maw of a fireplace, he stripped off slicker and hat while Broadrick kicked the door shut. The boom of the storm diminished to an endless muttering groan about the eaves, a table lamp thrust lanes of topaz light against the false shadows, and from some other part of the house rose a clatter of dishes. Broadrick rubbed his hands in front of him with a gusty, growling satisfaction and though there was now no need to raise his voice against the storm it had an unruly manner of smacking into the silence. "Mighty pleased to have you as a guest, Sheriff. Our trails have often crossed but this is my first pleasure of meetin' you in the flesh. Right ahead of you, sir, is the dinin'-room door."

The sheriff went through it and paused, at once becoming the target of a sudden scrutiny from eight men and a girl seated around the table; and as he stood there he seemed very little like a law officer who had spent the major part of his life in an exceedingly rough country. Dressed in neat black, he made a distinctly genteel, clerk-like appearance. Though tall, there was a worn fragility about him and the slight stoop of age. His wrists were thin, the hollows of neck and cheek considerably accented and a gaunt Adam's apple terminated a series of thoughtful features rendered almost melancholy by the presence of a drooping, silver-streaked mustache. A pair of mild blue eyes met the general stare diffidently and fell without seeming to have observed much of the scene.

"My crew," said Broadrick. "And my daughter, Marybelle. Boys, the sheriff. Be good now, blast you. Sheriff, the chair at my right."

McQuestion bowed slightly and sat down, observing the sharper interest of those at the table when his profession was mentioned. The girl sitting opposite him smiled and as this sudden light broke across her candid, boyish face there was a flash of spirit that at once

9

commanded McQuestion's instant adherence. She was no more than twenty, unmarked as yet by the sadness of the sheriff's world. Pale gold hair ran softly above fair temples; and in the firm, fresh lines of shoulder and breast was the hint of a vital fire that would one day burst from its prison. She spoke with a lilting, melody-making voice: "Who could be bad enough to bring you out in weather like this, Sheriff?"

"Outlaws," said the sheriff, "always pick poor weather."

"You're on that kind of business?" asked French Broadrick.

McQuestion marked the pause of sound at the table. And because he was by inclination a poker player on an errand requiring the finesse of poker strategy, he let his words fall distinctly into the calm: "I'm lookin' for a man who passed this way about a week ago, wearin' butternut britches and ridin' a stockin'-legged strawberry."

The deep silence held. There was no reaction from the men although Matt McQuestion's mild glance unexpectedly ranged down the table, no longer diffident. French Broadrick offered a platter of beef to the sheriff, still casually jovial. "What crime?"

"Murder," said the sheriff bluntly.

"Murder?" grunted Broadrick, easy humor

10

vanishing. "Murder, you say?" His big shoulders advanced on the sheriff. "Or justifiable homicide? There's a difference between the two things."

It was on the sheriff's tongue to explain the case but he checked the impulse. For he knew at that moment logic and instinct had made one of their infrequent unions. His man was on the ranch; more, his man was within the room. The knowledge came not from any overt signal or from the faces of the punchers who sat dull and stiff around him. It came from Marybelle Broadrick. At the word "murder" she flinched visibly. Her head came up and turned toward the crew, to be the next instant drawn back as if warned by an inner voice that this was betrayal. She stared now at McQuestion, plastic features losing color, rigidly still, and a mutely agitated query moving in her widening eyes. But this too was betrayal and she looked into her plate, hands withdrawn from the table.

French Broadrick spoke again, ruddy cheeks broken by concentric, scowling lines. "Murder or justifiable homicide, Sheriff?"

"Might be an argument in that," replied McQuestion, lying gravely. The girl's eyes lifted and touched him once more. He saw hope faintly replace bewilderment.

"What's his name?" pressed Broadrick.

11

"On the warrant it appears as John Doe."

"You don't know him?" said Broadrick, surprised.

"Never met the man. It's a blind chase after a stranger in the county. But the circumstantial evidence against him is mighty strong and there's a couple men who saw him from a distance when he was on the run."

"How in thunder do you expect to find him?" Broadrick wanted to know.

"One item is the horse."

"Which he could soon swap for another," countered Broadrick.

"The butternut pants," mused McQuestion.

"He's probably thrown 'em away," said Broadrick. "What's left? Nothing, it seems to me. I'd hate to start after a man on information as slim as that."

"One detail yet to mention," said the sheriff in a slowly casual manner that instantly tightened the interest of the room. "When we got to the scene there was the dead man, past tellin'. No witnesses and no messages. But a few feet from this dead man a dribble of blood ran along the rocks — no rain that day. The dribble went as far as some hoofprints. The hoofprints led away. You see? The dead man got in his shot before he fell and wherever this John Doe may be, he's packin' a hole in

12

him that won't wash off."

There was a brief, awkward silence. The girl ventured another straight, momentary glance toward Matt McQuestion and he detected a stiffening antagonism in her which at once strengthened his estimate of her character. She was partisan by nature and her loyalty, once fixed, would never waver. She would close her eyes and go unflinchingly the whole distance, to hell or to heaven.

So, at least, the sheriff guessed — and felt a more profound admiration for her. French Broadrick cleared his throat, staring above the heads of his men. "Well, that's enough to hook him up with the shootin'. But if nobody saw this affair, then nobody knows what brought it about or the justice of it. And you ain't caught your man yet, Sheriff."

"The trail," said McQuestion, quietly, "leads this way." His coffee was cold from stirring. All the while he had been exploring the table and at each successive glance he discarded one puncher and another from his mind. It took a certain toughness of fiber and a certain mental make-up to run with the wild bunch. Most of these fellows were middle-aged, plainly old retainers and lacking the impulses of a gun-toter. But a pair of younger men at the foot of the table increasingly interested him. One was a tall, slim character with deep red hair and a remarkably rippling coördination of muscle and nerve that expressed itself in each restless shift of his body. The other sat stolidly silent, dark and rugged and a fighter in every observable fiber. Contrasting the two, he heard French Broadrick bring the dinner to a curt close. "We'll go on with the work in the sheds this afternoon."

Rising with the rest, McQuestion let his eyes follow the crew out of a dining-room door as they filed into a rain-soaked yard. The red-haired man walked slowly and he took the descending steps with a faint stiffening of his carriage. The more rugged man brought up the rear; looking back, he caught the sheriff's glance and closed the door swiftly as he passed through. Somehow the gesture seemed almost protective of the red-head. McQuestion preceded his host into the living-room and put his back to the cheerful flames. The girl had disappeared. Broadrick moved aimlessly about the room, mind obviously struggling with a difficult thought. Presently he came to a stand in front of the sheriff, bluntly speaking: "You've told mighty little of the story. What's the rest of it?"

The blue glance of the sheriff narrowed against the firelight; still holding his place, he answered Broadrick: "In my life I've frequently had the disposition of some fellow's

14

future at my command. It's no easy thing to play the part of judge and I'll not say I always decided right. It weighs on me sometimes — the mistakes I made. I'm slower to act than I used to be. Any sucker can make an arrest. The difficult thing is to know when not to."

Broadrick's face was increasingly somber. "If this John Doe's what you say, where's the problem?"

"Unless I'm wrong he's not the only one to consider now," said the sheriff.

There was a quickening light in French Broadrick's eyes and a sudden ridging of face muscles. "I understand how you got your reputation. You're a lean old wolf, McQuestion."

McQuestion nodded, knowing then Broadrick grasped the situation. He knew, too, that whatever the final issue, Broadrick would never reveal the hunted man. It was one of the oldest laws of the range — sanctuary of a sort. If there was trouble, Broadrick was prepared to settle it in his own way, within the confines of the ranch. Comprehending this, McQuestion reached for his slicker and hat. "I'll be lookin' after my horse," he explained and passed back through the dining-room. When he stepped into the sheeting, tempestuous descent of rain he heard the girl's voice rising from another part of the house, troubled and high-pitched. The barn was straight ahead; left of it stood the bunkhouse in which the crew idled through noon. To the right of the barn and past the last outlying corrals he saw again that hillside compound where the loose stock was held; but, though his attention straightened on that area, the dull gloom of the day defeated his search for a stocking-legged strawberry. He entered the gray alley of the stable, found a section of clean burlap and proceeded to rub down his pony.

His chore was not done when he abandoned it, left the barn and walked toward the bunkhouse, through the windows of which glimmered a fogged, crystal lamplight. Opening the door with a preliminary rattle — he wanted no surprises yet — he went into quarters similar to a thousand others throughout the land.

A solid, rugged young man reared up from one of the lower bunks, bawling gravely: "Have a chair, sir."

"Thanks, but I'll stand," was McQuestion's courteous answer. "Been sittin' in leather all day long."

"And a poor day to travel," said the rugged one in the manner of a man making talk to be agreeable.

"Can't pick and choose," replied the sheriff, letting his glance stray. All the lower bunks were filled, but only one upper. That was occupied by the red-head, who lay sprawled on his back. The red-head stared above him, cigarette drooping from a lip corner, and without turning to the sheriff he spoke with a lazy, sardonic drawl:

"Outlaws should be more considerate of the constituted authorities."

"Well, Red," said the sheriff, "as long as they're considerate enough to leave tracks behind, I'm not carin' about the weather."

"Did this one?" queried Red, making no comment on the sheriff's application of a nickname.

"Yes."

"Mighty careless of him," mused Red. "Must of been a greenhorn."

"I'll know more about that later," said McQuestion, and then silence again descended upon the room — silence of men guarding their tongues.

"Time," said the rugged one, "to get back on the job."

He opened the door and went out, other punchers rising to follow slowly. Red rolled, put his feet over the edge of the bunk frame and let himself to the floor carefully, knees springing when he landed; and for a moment he faced the sheriff, grinning out of a wide, thin mouth. He was not handsome. The conformation of his face was too angular and his

17

eyes a too definite and unblinking green. But beneath the surface was a personality not to be mistaken, one at once restless, dominating, utterly self-certain. McQuestion caught the hard, unruffled competence behind that grin, and a lurking mockery.

"Was he a bad man at heart, Sheriff? Real bad?"

"I'm wonderin', Red," said the sheriff. "And I hope to find out."

Red turned casually and left the bunkhouse, a shadow of stiffness in his gait. McQuestion wheeled slowly where he stood, making a complete circle and taking in once more all that the room had to offer him. But it was an unnecessary move, for he knew then the identity of John Doe. "It's Red, for a certainty," he muttered. "The heavy boy with the good face is out of it."

But, strangely enough, the more or less definite end of his quest left him without the usual elation, without the hardening impulses preliminary to a capture. And as he paused in the open doorway another incident appeared through the weaving screen of rain to sway the even balance of his mind. Yonder on a side porch at the house Marybelle Broadrick stood beside Red, looking up to him and talking with swift gestures of her hands. Red was smiling. The smile broadened and he shook his head; one hand touched the girl's shoulder in a manner that seemed to the sheriff possessive and confident. The girl's body swayed back slightly and Red, turning, crossed the yard to an open shed. McQuestion, bent on having an answer to the increasing problem in his mind, ambled likewise to the shed and loitered there. An added hour or day didn't matter. There was such a thing as charity, even above justice, and that did matter. So, idling in the shed, he watched the working men with a patient interest.

In a kind of orderly confusion they were overhauling the ranch gear. At the forge one of the punchers bent livid iron over the anvil with swift, ringing strokes of his hammer. Another filed mower blades. The carpenter of the outfit ripped a board, saw whining into the anvil echoes. Meanwhile, the foreman had attacked a heavier chore. Pressing his back to a wagon frame, he began to lift, all his broad muscles swelling with the pressure. A helper stood by, attempting to slide a jack beneath the rising axle; but the weight was unwieldy and difficult to manage. Releasing his grip, the foreman looked about to find an unoccupied hand. His eyes touched the red-head slouching indolently at the forge and the sheriff saw the level features of the rugged one tighten up with a cool speculation. But it was only for a moment; the foreman called to another: "Bill, give me a hand here."

The red-head was aware of the fact that he had been passed by. The smiling irony of his face increased to a grin and he spoke to the crew generally: "Mighty muscles of our straw boss seem to grow weary."

"But not my tongue," observed the foreman, softly.

"Meanin' mine wags too much, uh?" murmured Red, grin widening. "Old son, you ought to be learnin' by now that muscle is cheap and brain rare. Anybody can sweat but blamed few can scheme well."

The appointed Bill came forward to help at the wagon, but the foreman stood still, features frowning on Red with an even-tempered concentration. "That may well be," he drawled. "But I'm inclined to wonder where the schemin' led. Consider it," he added gently, "as an idle question."

McQuestion turned from the shed and walked to the house, head bent against the rain and his blue glance kindling. "He could of asked Red to put a shoulder against that wagon. He could of made Red suffer with that game leg and let me catch on to the fact Red packed the injury. But he didn't because he's a dead sound sport. And how does Red pay back the compliment? By goadin' the foreman.

He understands he's safe on these premises and so he uses his sharp tongue to hurt. Reckless — and a mite of a fool. There's one crooked play to his credit but the chance is still open to him to go straight, if he wanted. Hard to tell how this girl, if he got her, would affect him. She might pull him right, but if she didn't he'd force her to his own sad level. He's got a glitter — and that attracts her now."

The living-room, when he reached it, was empty. Saddle-weary, he sank into a leather arm chair, and fell into a doze. When he woke the room was darker and the pound of the storm had increased. Out on the front porch voices rose, suppressed but still near enough for him to hear. The girl was talking swiftly: "I know you wouldn't give him away. You're not that kind, Lee. I only asked what you thought of him, now that the sheriff has told us the story."

"Why ask me?" countered the foreman's voice, blunt and angry. "What difference does it make to me? I'm not his keeper, and not yours."

"Lee, it means nothing to you? Look at me and say that!"

"One of us is a fool, Marybelle. I can look at you and say this much. I have played faithful Rover around here a long time. I seemed to get along fine until he came here. Not beefin' about it, either. If you like him it's your business. And you brought this up. Don't expect me to tattle on him."

The girl said: "I'm not fickle! I like him — but I want to know what men think of him. Lee, can't you understand a girl doubts her heart sometimes?"

"Better make up your mind. I'm not stayin' on the ranch if he does. We don't mix."

"Lee — you'd go! Would it be that easy for you?"

"Easy or hard, I'm not playin' faithful Rover any more. If you want him I'll not complain. But I ride — as soon as the sheriff leaves."

There was a prolonged silence, ended at last by the girl. "I never knew you cared that much, till now. Or that you cared at all. You have never spoken, Lee."

"Good lord, Marybelle! Where's your eyes?"

"Looking for something they couldn't find till this minute, Lee."

They moved away. McQuestion looked at his watch and found it beyond three. Rising, he picked up his hat and walked out into the gloom, adding fresh fuel to his thoughts. "The foreman was high card until Red came. The girl's troubled by his han'some manners. There's a little of the gambler in her and she catches the same thing in Red. But she ain't quite gone on him yet."

He came to an interested halt. A pair of men filed across the yard with a wagon tongue between them. The red-head held the front end of it, now limping obviously. Once he turned and called back to the other man, who twisted the tongue about to a different angle. The red-head slipped to his knees, dropped the tongue and ran back. There was a set rage on his cheeks, visible even through the murk, and his mouth framed some round, violent word. Deliberately he slapped the other man with both his palms and strode away. McQuestion withdrew, grumbling under his breath:

"So. He'll never soften up. That's the part the girl don't see. He'd destroy her, break her. What good's a bright mind if the heart's rotten?"

French Broadrick entered from the front, water cascading down his slicker. Marybelle came in from the kitchen, slim and graceful against the lamplight. Seeing her, Matt McQuestion's mind closed vault-like on all that he had learned this dismal afternoon. "I'm ridin'," said he, and moved toward his slicker.

"In this weather?" queried Broadrick. "Wait it out. Till mornin' anyhow."

"Spent too much time on a cold trail," said

McQuestion. "Should be back in Sun Ford this minute tendin' more necessary business. I'm grateful for your hospitality."

Broadrick's round face was strictured by inquisitive lines and he stood there surveying McQuestion like a man listening beyond the spoken words. Marybelle rested silent in the background.

"You asked me if it was justifiable homicide or murder," proceeded the sheriff. "I'll tell you. This John Doe was out in the hills tamperin' with somebody else's beef. A line rider heaves over the rim. John Doe does a natural thing — slings lead. He takes a bullet in reply but his first shot lands the line rider in the dirt. The line rider lies there, alive. John Doe does what only a natural and cold killer would do. Steppin' up close, he puts a second bullet into the back of the man's skull. Personally, I consider that murder. I bid you good day."

The girl's fists slowly tightened; a small sigh escaped her. McQuestion bowed and moved toward the dining-room, Broadrick following. Together they walked to the barn where McQuestion saddled. When the sheriff swung up and turned to leave the barn, Broadrick broke the long silence:

"You're a wolf, a gray old wolf. I don't get all this and I ain't goin' to try. But my next chore is to get your picture and hang it on my wall. So long, and the Lord bless you."

"See you sometime," said McQuestion, and rode into the yard. The foreman was at that minute leaving the shed and McQuestion swerved to intercept the man and to lean down.

"My boy," he said, "forty-one years ago I lost a girl because I was mighty proud and stiff. Along came another man who had the grace to speak his piece. And I've been a little lonesome ever since. You've got to tell the ladies what they want to hear. Adios."

Well away from the house, he turned from his due northern course, broke into a steady run and cut about the little valley, through heavy timber and across rugged defiles. Half an hour later, he arrived at a road coursing to the south — the exit from Broadrick's as well as the exit from the county. There was, a few rods above the road, a tumbled confusion of rocks. He placed his horse behind them, dismounted and crawled to an uncomfortable station beside the road.

"Man never knows," he grumbled, "whether his monkeyin' with the course of fated events is wise or not. And —"

He raised his rifle, training it on a figure suddenly coming around a near bend from the Broadrick ranch. Fifty yards closer the rider became Red, who advanced slackly on a stocking-legged strawberry horse. McQuestion turned the safety of his rifle and cast a metallic, thin order through the wind:

"Hands up — and sudden!"

Red reined in, made a confused move toward his gun, saw nothing for a target, and reached to the leaking heavens.

"Get down — put your back to me — lift your gun gently and throw it behind!"

Again Red obeyed. McQuestion rose and walked forward. The red-head twisted his head, recognized the sheriff then, and wrenched his whole body about. The reckless face broke into long lines of passion. "Sheriff! How'd you figger this?"

McQuestion paused, all adrip. Nothing showed clear between hat brim and slicker collar but two blue eyes. "I've done this for thirty years, Red. I ought to know. Broadrick wouldn't betray you. But after what I told him, I was pretty sure he'd never tolerate you another minute on the ranch. He'd give you your horse and tell you to lope. Which way would you travel? South, because that's out of the county and opposite the direction you saw me go."

The red-head shook with greater fury; the blaze of his eyes grew hotter, brighter, half crazed. "Damn you — damn you forever! You

26

lied about me! I never put a second shot in that line rider's skull! That's what stuck in Broadrick's craw! He believed it and he couldn't stand it! And the girl stared at me like I was a monster! I'll kill you for that lie — before God I will!"

"Yeah," said the sheriff, "I lied. But I gave you an even break — until you belted that puncher in the face for twistin' your bad leg. Then I knew what you'd do to the girl if you ever got her. There's a better man left behind to take care of Marybelle. So I lied. Still, I think the ample folds of justice will cover it. Say adios to the land, Red. Say adios. You'll see it no more."

Court Day

As soon as the train dropped him, Sheriff Sudden Ben Drury walked up the street through his own heavy cigar smoke to the marshal's office in the courthouse. Emerett Bulow was marshal of Prairie City that year.

Sudden Ben said: "Howard Durbin came before the grand jury at Two Dance yesterday and presented information against one Conrad Weiser on the charge of murder. The grand jury returned a secret indictment. Where do I find Weiser?"

Bulow murmured: "He's a homesteader fifteen miles down the Silver Bow."

Against Bulow, who was a six-footer with pale blue eyes and a flat-boned face, Sudden Ben Drury cut a rather small figure. He was a carefully dressed man and a shrewd one, having spent the best of twenty years dealing with the politics of a turbulent county. The sense of that knowledge was grained into his smooth cheeks; it was to be detected in the easy affability of his manner. He seemed soft, but this was only part of that outward show, for no man could long be peace officer of Sage

29

County unless there was grit in him somewhere. The news obviously disturbed Emerett Bulow and the sheriff, observing this, was quick to ask: "They got a good case against Weiser?"

Bulow remained silent a long while, as though searching for the exact thing to say. It seemed to come hard, as most speech did for this rather unimaginative town marshal. "Good enough, I suppose. They found Arizona Matt a mile from Weiser's place. He had a bullet in his head. He was one of Howard Durbin's riders."

Sudden Ben's eyes were gray and smart and half hidden by the cigar smoke. He said dryly: "What else?"

"The situation," added Emerett Bulow in his dour way, "is kind of bad here. The hoemen keep a-comin' in to settle up the Silver Bow flats. It's busted up the flats entirely as free range. The cattlemen are all pushed back into the hills, and they're pretty sore." It wasn't an explanation and Sudden Ben held his peace until Emerett Bulow added more reluctantly than before: "Con Weiser is a sort of head man among the homesteaders."

The sheriff removed his cigar and tapped the ashes and returned it securely to his lips. There wasn't any need to ask more, for this was still a county run for and by cattle. The sheriff held his office by virtue of beef, and so did the marshal. They looked at each other in long silence, knowing how it was.

"What kind of a man is this Weiser?"

"Why," said Bulow, "not bad at all. I'll go with you."

So presently they were riding out of Prairie in a buggy, with the high flash of a July sun fully beating against them and the flats running all tawny and powder-dry into the south. Seven miles from town the road reached the hundred-foot canyon of the winding Silver Bow and subsequently followed it. This was on to the left. To the right, a mile away, low foothills lifted up. All along the river bluff nesters' small shacks began to show.

"Not a settler here two years ago," commented the sheriff. "Nothin' but Durbin's cattle and Hugh Dan Lake's cattle and the Custer Company's cattle. Times sure change."

"There'll be trouble."

"Maybe," said the sheriff quietly, "I better come out this way more often," and his eyes were narrowed and full of thought behind the continuing cloud of his cigar smoke. Fifteen miles from town Emerett Bulow drove the buggy into Con Weiser's yard. The family had seen the dusty signals of the buggy from afar and now was lined up against the side of the house.

"Con," said Emerett Bulow, in a regretting voice, "this is Sheriff Drury. I'm sorry." And afterward he put his hands across his knees, leaving the bad news to the sheriff.

The sheriff let the silence go on, laying a sharp and close glance across the interval to the man standing by the house. Weiser was a German of the thin and dark type, turning gray and stooped at the shoulders from work. His attention came back to the sheriff, black and bitter. Sudden Ben weighed him carefully, searching him for the prospects of trouble. After twenty years of man-hunting, he knew this first contact was always the most dangerous. Some men were cool, and some went mad. But presently he had removed his cigar and was speaking with an easy courtesy.

"I don't like to do this, but if you'll get in with Emerett and me we'll drive to Prairie."

Weiser said: "I been expectin' it," and turned through the doorway into the house.

Relaxed in his seat, his glance scanning the family, yet never quite leaving that door's yawning square — he saw Weiser's wife let her formless shoulders droop. She was Old German and misery was in her eyes, but she wouldn't speak. Four children of an in-between age were grouped closely together, as wooden as if they had been told to pose for a picture. An older child stood at the edge of his vision, near the house's corner. Venturing a direct glance that way, Sudden Ben forgot the doorway.

She was Weiser's daughter, he realized for she had the same definite mold of features. She was slim and about eighteen and her face was as clear and proud as any the sheriff had ever seen in the rough wastes of his county; and though the breath of fear touched this yard there was no fear in her. Sudden Ben held her glance a moment and then whipped his interest back to Con Weiser, now coming out the door. There had been that moment of negligence on Sudden Ben's part, leaving its faint shock in him.

Weiser got into the buggy, saying nothing to his family. Emerett Bulow turned the team and drove quickly away, with a deeper and deeper gloom on his face. And then a quick tattoo of a horse turned all three of them in the seat and they watched the girl gallop out of the Weiser yard, bound away into the lower flats. The news, Sudden Ben guessed would travel soon enough. Con Weiser was humped forward in the narrow seat, indifferent and without speech.

It went so all the way back to Prairie. As soon as they came to town Bulow took Weiser to the jail room in the courthouse and Sudden Ben, having two hours to kill before train time, methodically set about paying visits to Prairie's shops and shopkeepers, genially shaking hands all along the route and thereby building up his political fences. Afterward, he crossed to Mike Danahue's saloon and was closeted there a half-hour. It was the saloonmen in Sage County who knew the drifts of public sentiment, and who possessed power.

Emerett Bulow accompanied him later to the train. Gloom rode the marshal's words. "There's going to be hell to pay."

Sudden Ben nodded, having already learned as much from Mike Danahue in the saloon. "Think you can keep Weiser safe until the trial?"

The marshal was touchy about that. "I never lost a man out of my jail yet and I'm too old to begin the habit. The hoemen won't free him and the cattle boys won't lynch him."

"I'll be back for the trial," Sudden Ben assured him and went into the smoking car. Settled deeply in the plush seat he watched the dun earth scud by. Ashes fell on his vest and he seemed asleep. Yet his shrewd mind, packed with the lore of the land and the ways of its men, was closely analyzing the imponderables of Con Weiser's arrest. The cattlemen, he knew, were making a test of their strength against the rising tides of settlers. It didn't make any difference whether Con

Weiser was guilty or not. Con Weiser was only a symbol. Trouble would come of it as Bulow had said.

The train took him away from Prairie City at three o'clock. At four o'clock Tip Mulvane, with a thousand miles of riding behind him, came into Prairie and put up his horse at Orlo Torvester's stable.

As a stranger in a distant land, Tip Mulvane followed his instincts and his long training in trouble. He kept still. Sleeping and eating and idling out the days on the shaded hotel porch, his eyes saw and his ears heard. He was a long-shaped man and it was plain to see that he belonged on a horse; for even when he walked there was that faint straddling gait of the rider. His eyes were a gunpowder gray, sometimes almost black when the sun didn't touch them, and his bones were flat and big, and weather had smoothed his face and disciplined it to a saddle-brown inexpressiveness. He was not more than twenty-five but Emerett Bulow, who had watched him with a growing interest from his first appearance, knew that somewhere he had been seasoned and toughened beyond his years. It was to be seen in the slow, careful way Tip Mulvane looked at this town.

So when the trial of Con Weiser took up, Tip Mulvane knew all he needed to know.

The story was clear and the ending already foretold. Standing in the back of the crowded courtroom on the second day of debate, he understood what the verdict would be. He had only to look at the double row of faces in the jury box and guess it; for those were the faces of range riders and not of hoemen, and he knew their kind to the very core. One of the Durbin riders sat in the witness seat and was wearily answering the questions of Con Weiser's young and fretful lawyer. Con Weiser rested in a camp chair beneath the judge, with his hands folded, showing no interest at all. Weiser, Tip Mulvane decided, knew the answer, too. Heat filled the room. Emerett Bulow and the county's sheriff, Sudden Ben, stood at the far edge of the judge's bench.

The trial had dragged its way through the morning without excitement, yet Tip Mulvane could feel the quality of trouble growing. It was like the pressure of an arm against him; and when Howard Durbin, one of the three great ranchers in the valley and the employer of the dead rider, got up to leave the room that pressure stiffened and an unspoken rage whirled up from the homesteaders crowded so gauntly and bitterly against the back wall of the room. They blocked the door and when Durbin got there they didn't move. Tip Mulvane's gray eyes registered that little scene attentively. Durbin stopped, a slim and arrogant man with the sense of power written in every gesture, and he looked at those nesters blocking his way until at last some of them stirred and let him through. Tip Mulvane said to himself, with a touch of admiration, "He's nervy," and then heard the judge's gavel announce noon recess. He shuffled out of the courthouse with the crowd.

Sunlight laid its hard and yellow flash all along Prairie's street. The hitch racks were crowded with teams and saddle ponies and people now rolled in a slow tide beneath the board awnings, not talking much. The feeling had been bad all morning; it was getting worse, with more homesteaders crowding into town and collecting in small groups up and down the dusty way. Durbin's punchers and the riders of Hugh Dan Lake and of the Custer Land and Cattle Company made their headquarters in Mike Danahue's saloon — strictly aloof from the hoemen.

Tip Mulvane stopped opposite the courthouse, watching all this with a cool and attentive eye. The sudden, acute hunger of an active man was upon him, but he waited there, not quite knowing why until Katherine Weiser came out of the courthouse door and turned toward the porch of the hotel where other homesteaders' women had collected. There was, at once, some meaning to his standing so idly in the hot summer's sun. A tall young German settler with very blond hair was with her, but she seemed to Tip Mulvane just then to be alone on this dusty street. It was in the swing of her slim body and the straight and proud turning of her shoulders. Once she looked over the street and he caught the fair, composed glance that touched him for a brief moment and passed on.

There were hoemen behind Tip Mulvane and he heard one of them say: "If Kitty Weiser was a man I'd be sorry to be in Howard Durbin's shoes."

Somebody said quietly: "There's other men to do it."

Tip Mulvane sauntered indolently along the dust, not knowing he made a puzzle to Emerett Bulow and Sudden Ben Drury standing under the gallery of Mike Danahue's saloon. Sudden Ben's eyes followed Tip Mulvane with a narrowing brightness. He said to Emerett Bulow: "Who's that?"

"Stranger come to town."

"Like a man I might have seen somewhere," murmured Sudden Ben and watched Tip Mulvane turn into the little restaurant down by the depot.

Tip Mulvane ate his meal and sat a moment at the stool, shaping himself a cigarette and

38

listening to the talk that ran its brief, half-sullen undertone around him; and later he went back up the street and laid the edge of his shoulder against a street post, and so stood there. A line of hoemen blackened by the prairie sun sat at the edge of the walk, their talk low and brief — and more and more bitter. It was a constant tone in Tip Mulvane's ears while he watched people return to the courthouse. Howard Durbin came from the hotel and stopped to light up a cigar. Old Hugh Dan Lake, the valley's most powerful cattleman, strolled up and stopped to talk to Durbin; and then Durbin beckoned with a finger and two Durbin riders came from the saloon and listened to what he said, and walked back again. A spray of fine wrinkles appeared at each corner of Tip Mulvane's eyes to indicate the quality of his interest just then; and his glance measured Howard Durbin from top to toe and found something that sent a faint constricting motion across the breadth of his lips.

Sudden Ben Drury appeared from the courthouse and went directly to where Durbin and Hugh Dan Lake stood. Sudden Ben spoke to them, and Howard Durbin shook his head instantly, as though the sheriff's talk had been presumptuous. There was, Tip Mulvane could see, no thought of concession in Howard

Durbin; the man was driving on for a fight, very certain of its outcome.

A homesteader left the courthouse and advanced on the homesteaders gathered in front of Tip Mulvane. This man's stringy shoulders were hiked up and his eyes looked a little wild. "It won't get to the jury today." A puncher whirled into town and passed the grouped homesteaders with a sidewise stare that was openly insolent, and dismounted in front of the saloon; and suddenly the cattle hands made a silent group yonder and the hoemen made a sullen crowd opposite — with a gulf as deep and as wide as the ocean lying between.

At the head of the street, beyond the courthouse, a few men began idly firing at a target to pass the time, the gunfire echoes riving the heated air like huge wedges. Katherine Weiser walked from hotel to courthouse, her black hair shining in the sullen light. She passed Howard Durbin without glancing at him, but Durbin's head wheeled around and his stare followed her boldly and with a frank appraisal. Tip Mulvane's long body stirred and his lids crept more closely together while he watched Howard Durbin's face. Faint anger turned him restless. He pivoted from the hoemen, his spurs jingling along the boardwalk. All the cattle hands were in front of Mike Danahue's and they watched him advance upon the saloon, their expressions inscrutably blank. His own glance raked them indolently and then he passed into the saloon, got a bottle and a glass and walked to a table and sat down.

He had his drink and sat with his shoulders sliding down against the chair's back, waiting for the whisky to cut the edge of that hard and careful alertness which had guarded his life for so long. Certain things he saw here with the over-distinct vision of a man who knew the ways of trouble too well. Howard Durbin and the other big cattle owners were riding this affair hard. They had Con Weiser, the chief man of the homesteaders, in jail and they seemed to feel that the homesteaders would not rise to fight back. It was, Tip Mulvane conceded, smart reasoning. For he had watched those brown, slow-voiced sod-busters all during the week and could see nowhere a fire that would explode their angers. They needed a fighter to rouse them, and had none.

A faint impulse stirred his nerves and began to lay pressure along his muscles. He straightened in the chair and said to himself, "Be careful." He knew what was going on in him then and regretted it. Far back in Montana that same impulse had led him into trouble; it was why he had put a thousand miles behind him — to escape the consequences of an Irish tem-

41

per that would not let him alone, a temper that took the injustices done to others as personal affronts. This was his weakness and this was why he ran before the wind now. "I have," he thought, "got to get out of here. Been here too long." His face, at this moment, was smooth and studious.

The long day rolled on while he sat there. Durbin men tramped in and out of the place and presently people were coming from the courthouse, the street boards sounding to their weight. The sun had gone down. A train whistle had looed its hoarse way across the windless air, and a supper triangle began to go wing-a-ding-a-wing-a-ding" from the hotel.

He rose then and strolled directly to the stable. He said to the hostler, "I'll be leavin' right after I eat," and made his way down to the restaurant near the depot.

There was a glass-clear, sunless light in the world for a little while; and afterward dusk dropped down in deep powder-gray layers, drowning out the prairie's far reaches. This was the hour of peace; yet, cruising up the street later toward the stable, he felt an old restlessness beating its tom-tom in him. Lights began to throw their long lanes across the dusk, turning that dusk to a melted silver. He paced on by the stable, though he had intended to go in and ride away from Prairie forever.

Beyond town he saw the dusty strip of road undulate luminously southward toward the Silver Bow, with a low moon throwing its pale gush down upon the long-rolling land. On his right the shapes of a cemetery's headboards laid their faint rows before him; and then he saw a woman standing there beside the road, and he heard her crying.

Softly, as though she were ashamed of tears. But that sound was, to Tip Mulvane's volatile sympathy, like the clap of thunder. It stopped him dead and wheeled him half around. All at once the crying stopped and the woman turned to him with a gesture like defense and he saw it to be Katherine Weiser.

He removed his hat instantly, a deep wonder having its way with him. Through the week he had watched her from afar, the simplicity of her manner and the depth of her calm as arresting to him as a tall pillar of fire shining through a dark night. It was the contrast which hit him so hard now. Her calm was gone.

He said: "What would you want a man to do for you?"

He heard her breath lift and stop, and fall out. Her chin rose and her face was slim and proud and not easily stirred by strangers. She looked at him, no expression there for him to understand. That deep calm controlled her voice when she spoke: "It is beyond your help."

He said candidly: "Why do you figure I have stayed in this town for a week?"

She was listening quietly to the question; she was thinking about it while the moments went by. And then she said, "I have wondered," and turned back toward town. He watched her straight body stir against the town lights, the smell of dust and sage and summer-cured forage grasses rising keenly to his nostrils. The sound of her voice remained in his head, like the memory of a bell that had chimed one melodious note.

He waited until she had entered town before moving. Afterward his long legs carried him in half-haste back to the stable. He said to the hostler, "I have changed my mind," and crossed directly to the courthouse. The marshal's office was at the back end of the building, with a light shining through its open door. Tip Mulvane ducked his head by habit as he passed into the room. Emerett Bulow had been walking around the desk; he stopped and showed Tip Mulvane a morose and half-belligerent expression. Sudden Ben sat with his feet on the desk's top, cigar smoke heavily concealing his expression. Yet it was to Sudden Ben that Tip Mulvane paid his strictest attention. Sudden Ben's eyes showed a faint gleam through the smoke.

Mulvane said: "I'd like to see this Con Weiser a minute."

Emerett Bulow grumbled: "Nobody's seein' Weiser."

Sudden Ben drawled: "Let him go up, Emerett."

Emerett Bulow scowled and thought about it in his long-drawn way. In the end he nodded to Mulvane and swung through another door and tramped up a dismal flight of stairs to the second floor. The light of a bracket lamp threw a sallow glow along a narrow corridor. Coming by Bulow, Tip Mulvane faced the grillwork of a cell and saw Con Weiser seated on the edge of a bunk behind the grillwork. Bulow said, "You got five minutes," and paced backward ten feet and waited like that.

The light was against Con Weiser's eyes. He couldn't see Tip Mulvane. He said, without getting up: "Who is that?" There was a dead, indifferent calm in the man's voice. He was small and dark-skinned, with tight lips and a gray and bitter expression in his eyes. He didn't hope for much. Mulvane said: "Like to ask you a question."

"No more questions," stated Weiser. "It is no use how I answer. The result will be the same. Who are you?"

"It makes a difference to me," murmured

Tip Mulvane. "You kill this fellow?"

"You are a fool," said Con Weiser. But long afterward he added indifferently: "There were plenty reasons for him to die, and plenty of men who could have done it. But I didn't. In a land run by cattlemen I know better than to make trouble. But whether I did or didn't, it makes no difference. You go look at that jury and you will see what I mean."

"That's all," said Emerett Bulow from the background.

Tip Mulvane went down the stairs and came suddenly upon the full and interested weight of Sudden Ben's glance. The sheriff had lowered his cigar; he had drawn his feet from the desk, and now sat forward in his chair. He said: "Just travelin' through?" Emerett Bulow walked across the room so that he could have his look at Tip Mulvane's face.

"Just travelin'," agreed Mulvane.

"Tryin' to recall if I've met you somewhere," murmured the sheriff.

"No," said Mulvane. "Montana's my home."

"Big country to be from," judged the sheriff.

"Yes," said Tip Mulvane, and left the room. Silence held on here long after he had gone. Emerett Bulow cleared his throat, his mind toiling its way painfully toward a new thought. "You suppose the hoemen have hired that fellow to do a little professional shootin'?"

Sudden Ben's eyes were bright with speculation. Shrewdness showed itself all along his face. "No," he decided. "But I'd guess he could shoot."

"It wouldn't take much to set off those nesters."

It was a thing Sudden Ben had been debating all during the week. He said: "They're a slow bunch. They'll fight but they don't flame up easy, like cowhands. They need somebody to set off the spark — and they don't have anybody since this Con Weiser's in the jug."

"Trouble's comin'," stated Emerett Bulow. "You wait till that jury turns in its verdict."

"It may come," assented Sudden Ben. "Howard Durbin is ridin' this thing hard." A sudden impulse compelled him to clap on his hat and leave the room. For a little while he stood in a patch of shadow and watched the street with the careful eye of one who had spent his life analyzing and predicting the vagaries of human behavior. He was the product of a fenceless, free cattle land and all his sympathies were with the old order. Yet the intimations of change both disturbed and warned him in the shape of those homesteaders who tramped the walks of this street so solemnly. They had a power they didn't realize; and the day would come when they

47

would control this land. He was smart enough to see that, and human enough to regret it, and politician enough to adjust himself to it. Passing toward the hotel he saw the homesteaders knotted up around Orlo Torvester's stable, not talking much. Mike Danahue's saloon was full of Durbin's and Hugh Dan Lake's riders, and all the elements of an explosion lay in Prairie, waiting for the fatal spark. Pushing into the hotel he walked directly over the lobby and let himself into a back room where he knew Durbin and old Hugh Dan Lake would be.

They were at a table, with a bottle of good whisky between them. A third man, Gray Lovewell of the Custer Land and Cattle Company, was here also. It was this trinity which held the key to the situation. Sudden Ben stirred the layered cigar smoke with an idle gesture of his arm. All three looked at him, and he could see they wouldn't listen. But he said:

"You boys are a little too sure."

"Let the jury decide," said Howard Durbin, almost scornfully. Lamplight struck the square face of his diamond ring and flashed up a brilliant gleaming.

"It's your jury," pointed out Sudden Ben frankly. "I'm saying you'd better drop it word to change its vote."

Old Hugh Dan Lake's face caught a scarlet ruddiness. Howard Durbin stared at the sheriff with a smiling insolence. "Ben," he said, "you have suited me perfectly as a sheriff. But don't go currying favor with those damned rascals breaking up an honest cattleman's range."

Sudden Ben's eyes were gray and smart. He drawled: "You don't see it, but times change. That Silver Bow country is lost to you. It's a thing you'd better recognize. It would be good business if you'd make a dicker with those hoemen. The flats to them and the bench country to you. Or you may lose both."

"No," said Howard Durbin. "I'll break that bunch."

"For a man using government land without title," said Sudden Ben, "you're a little proud. It don't do no harm to use reason."

"I'll run 'em out," said Durbin vigorously.

Sudden Ben turned to the door and opened it. He looked back a moment, murmuring, "That's what a fellow said about grasshoppers once," and then left.

Up in a room of the Prairie House Tip Mulvane sat before a small table, building up a pile of matches aimlessly, his eyes half closed and a cigarette sagging at the corner of his long lips.

He was standing across from the courthouse

— and had been there an hour — when a man came out and crossed to the little knot of homesteaders. Tip Mulvane heard the man say: "Case won't go to the jury until afternoon."

A homesteader said: "They ain't foolin' anybody. That jury had its instructions when it was sworn in."

Tip Mulvane saw all their brown and bitter faces making a swarthy shine in the sunlight. They were slow-tempered men and they were stung by the injustice of Con Weiser's trial, yet there was nobody to set fire to that anger. Marksmen were again banging away at a target beyond the courthouse and presently the homesteaders drifted in that direction, leaving Tip Mulvane alone by Orlo Torvester's stable. Durbin's cattle hands were sitting back in the gallery shade by Danahue's saloon.

It was eleven-thirty then, and a moment later Katherine Weiser came from the courthouse and walked toward the hotel, with the big blond German lad dutifully beside her. For an instant she saw Tip Mulvane across the dust and was aware of him, and during that moment all else on this bright and dusty street faded, as though a fog closed down upon the edges of his vision. She was a straight and resolute shape moving along the boardwalk with a rhythm that struck some deep response in his brain. Pride held her steady against the eyes of this town. That was what hit him — this courage to show the world a steady face. She went on into the hotel's doorway and a feeling of regret washed through Tip Mulvane, the regret a man would feel at the vanishing of light from an unfamiliar trail. But before entering she had turned and thrown one quick look back to him. It was the look of a woman who wanted to see and wanted to be seen.

Mulvane tipped his head and his long body swayed away from the gallery post. He was thinking, "I ought to get aboard that horse and go." Yet he knew then he wouldn't. It was, he thought wistfully, his manner to pitch himself into troubles that held no profit for him. The firing lifted beyond the courthouse and on impulse he strolled that way. There were fifteen or twenty nesters standing around a pair of marksmen who idly tried their skill at a tin can ninety feet out on the prairie.

He watched dust jet up after each shot, a critical indifference possessing him; and he noted how awkwardly the two nesters lifted and sighted their guns. Afterward he moved through the crowd until he stood beside these two. One of them had lifted his revolver for another deliberate sight. Tip Mulvane said, "You're wasting your lead," and wheeled his own gun from its holster in one short revolving motion. Sound howled into the hot day and the flittering can ninety feet away rolled and bounced at each bullet's impact and then dropped into a yonder coulee. Tip Mulvane holstered his gun and turned about to find all those brown and patient and inexpressive faces showing him whole-hearted interest.

He said: "Leave the .45 to the riders. It is their gun and you can't beat 'em at it. You boys are shotgun people. A shotgun is a deadly thing anywheres on this street. What the hell you standing back for?"

He wanted no answer and waited for none. Walking back toward the stable at a long, impatient stride he felt an old wildness slowly fill the empty spaces of his body. Suddenly, after a thousand miles of drifting, after a long summer's loneliness, the world was fresh again and life held a color and richness for him. He could not help this. The kickback of the gun against his arm had been a shock to revive a Tip Mulvane he had thought buried in Montana.

There was no more firing up the street. Durbin's punchers, attracted by the sudden wicked burst of his gun, were out in the street, watching him wheel and take stand by Orlo Torvester's stable. The homesteaders were trooping in. And afterward people began to come from the courthouse, released by noon recess. Howard Durbin and Hugh Dan Lake stood beneath the shelter of the hotel's board awnings. The jury appeared in the street, shepherded by Emerett Bulow, and walked double file toward the hotel for dinner.

It was like this, with the street crowded and all eyes focused on the jury pacing toward the hotel, when Tip Mulvane dropped his cigarette into the dust and ground it beneath his foot and crossed over to where Howard Durbin stood. Nothing showed on his cheeks and the sudden brightness of his eyes was half stifled by the closing edges of his lids. He came to the far walk and swung toward Howard Durbin, walking without haste. The jury was fifteen feet away, and coming on; and the weight of attention slowly swung to that little spot in front of the hotel's door. Howard Durbin made a definite stand on the walk, his position careless and arrogant there as though the world could step around him for all he cared.

Tip Mulvane said: "You like this spot?"

Howard Durbin wheeled about in one astonished motion and a sudden anger flamed up and showed through his eyes. He said, "What —" and said no more. For the town's indrawn attention was fully upon this scene now and Tip Mulvane, calculating coolly what it would mean, drove his high shoulder into Howard Durbin's chest and lifted his arms and spun Durbin around and threw him bodily out into the dust. Durbin made one long, wild turning motion with his arms spread-eagled to the hot sky and fell thus grotesquely to the earth.

Shock stunned this town like the enormous strike of thunder. The jury had frozen to a still, double row on the walk. All the homesteaders were bronze statues at the edge of Tip Mulvane's vision and there was no motion over by the saloon where Durbin's punchers had taken root. He heard the hard rise and fall of old Hugh Dan Lake's breathing at his right hand; and then he closed all that out of his mind and, remotely smiling, watched Howard Durbin rise from the dust.

Tall and pale and with a yellow blaze of rage in those sulky, handsome eyes, he said, in a choking voice: "Step into the street! Step away from those women!"

Out of the ranks of the punchers came a sudden warning: "Careful, Howard. I saw him use a gun."

"Step out into the street!" cried Durbin.

Motion swayed the homesteaders in the background like wind ruffling wheat. Somebody yelled and at once more homesteaders charged from Torvester's stable and up the street. A shotgun exploded, its shot rattling high on Torvester's stable wall. A woman screamed and Durbin's punchers came alive and began to spread over the dust. A homesteader's huge shape drove forward, straight toward the punchers, and then all those brawny bitter men broke like a wave and crashed on against the punchers by Danahue's saloon. The shotgun boomed again and afterward Sudden Ben's voice cut its knifelike warning through the howl: "There's women here!" No more gunfiring sounded; but the homesteaders raced on and Howard Durbin went down under that wave and the punchers vanished in its whirl and the howl got greater and the beat of the hoemen's fists made dull, meaty echoes against the targeted Durbin men. The jury had vanished and Emerett Bulow had vanished, and Sudden Ben and Hugh Dan Lake were gone.

Tip Mulvane held his position, watching Howard Durbin rise to his knees and go down again under the full lunge of an on-racing homesteader's heavy boot. Durbin rolled in the dust and came up like a cat and was struck and turned and struck once more. Sudden Ben appeared in the melee and seized Durbin's shoulder and pushed him against the tide, on toward the courthouse. The courthouse bell was ringing. A team bolted from the hitch rack and raced out of town; and the homesteaders were breaking into little knots as they met the Durbin punchers. Ten-gallon hats rolled along the ground and Danahue's windows crashed and inside that place the furious echoes of wreckage arose.

Tip Mulvane moved across the street, pushing men aside with the flats of his hands. He walked into Torvester's stable and found the hostler crouched gloomily there. He said, "I guess I'll use my horse now."

"You've played hell," said the hostler bitterly. "The hoemen have got this town now!"

Tip Mulvane saddled and stood up in the leather and pointed his horse out. The heavy sound of fighting had fallen away. Something crashed massively in Danahue's saloon and here and there men cried out. Somebody came up the street on the run, bent well over. The hostler said again: "The dam' hoemen —"

Tip Mulvane looked at the hostler, smiling with a gentleness and a sadness. "Sure, I know. It's tough to see the old days go."

"Then why in God's name you put in your oar —"

Tip Mulvane laughed outright. He said, "Brother, I wish I knew." Across the street he saw Sudden Ben march out of the courthouse with Con Weiser and Howard Durbin. Emerett Bulow hove into sight and Hugh Dan

56

Lake appeared from the hotel. They made a little group in the harsh sunlight, with Sudden Ben pointing his finger at one and another of those men, in the peacemaker's role. Tip Mulvane rode from the stable and turned southward bound down the Silver Bow. The sheriff saw him and came at once into the street. He said, "Friend, wait." But Tip Mulvane's eyes went backward to the hotel, seeing Katherine Weiser framed in the doorway yonder. The big blond youth was advancing toward her and Tip could see the girl's smile go out to him. Then the smile had gone and her dark glance came down the street and touched Tip, and stayed there.

"Friend," said the sheriff, "don't I know you?"

"No," said Tip Mulvane. But the question sank in and found its mark. He added quietly: "Well, maybe you do. The world is full of strays like me."

The sheriff put up his hand. He said: "Somewhere in this world you made big tracks. It has been a satisfaction to me to watch you. So long," and shook Tip Mulvane's hand. Tip Mulvane lifted the reins and started to go, and looked behind him once more. Katherine Weiser's glance met him, dark and steady. The German lad was beside her. She spoke to him and her hand touched his chest, pushing him away, and afterward she took one step forward and looked at Tip Mulvane in the way of a woman who wanted to see — and to be seen. Tip Mulvane lifted his hat and cantered away.

A short way from town he reined in. In the south the land lay yellow and smoky. Far, far down that way lay another thousand miles of travel. He was thinking of the campfires to be lighted along that trail and the howl of the coyotes on other lonely hillsides. There was, he thought, never any end to the trail for a man like him. He folded his hands on the saddle's horn and considered them with heavy thought. "I am running from a shadow. But the shadow is right in front of me now and always will be."

He looked behind him once more and saw dust smoke rising from a wagon coming out of town, following this Silver Bow trail toward the homestead settlement. It would be, he guessed, the Weiser family bound homeward. Excitement brightened the powder-gray glance and afterward he remembered the manner in which Katherine Weiser had pushed the German boy away. It was an omen. He thought, "If I stay here it will never be dull — and never lonely," and reined in the pony, waiting motionlessly there for the wagon to catch up.

Officer's Choice

Night had settled down on the prairie. Through the darkness a horse and rider moved slowly toward the soft glimmering lights of a town, entered it, stopped at a building.

The building was a stable. From it, presently, a man emerged. A hostler. The rider dismounted and addressed the man; his tones were those of one accustomed to command.

"Water my horse, please. And give him plenty of hay — but no oats."

"Yes, sir," the man replied. And, since strangers were always a source of interest and potential excitement in Lost Eagle, he observed the newcomer carefully.

The rider took a cigar from his pocket, which instantly removed him from the hostler's classification of average hand, and struck a match to the tip. Under a large felt hat was the outline of a ruddy, weather-swept face, the gleam of silvered temples and the flash of drill-straight eyes. Then the match flickered out.

"Anything else?" inquired the hostler with a touch of deference.

"Thanks, no," said the rider, curtly polite. His glance shifted along the street. Directly opposite was a saloon, bright and noisy; adjoining it stood a building whose second-story windows were framed with iron gratings and above the roof of which projected a bell tower. His attention paused there.

"Sheriff's office," offered the hostler, hoping to sweep up a few crumbs of information.

The rider's laconic "Thanks" came over departing shoulders. He crossed the street, lowered his head beneath the office door lintel and stepped inside. A man stood in the center of a dim, barren room; a rugged man with the air of patience on him. All along the walls were the signs of the man-hunter's trade: reward notices, warnings, rogues' gallery pictures; and, in one corner, a grave little girl sat on a packing box, quite still.

"My apologies," said the rider. "I'm looking for Sheriff Cliff McLean."

"My name," replied the sheriff, soberly cordial. He nodded at a chair. "Sit down."

The little girl frowned thoughtfully and pointed to a star pinned on her dress. "I won't arrest you."

The sheriff grinned, upon which the heaviness of his face fell away. He reached across for the star, unpinning it with fingers that were both clumsy and gentle. "Past your bedtime, ma'am. And no more remarks from the gallery. You'll scare my cash customers."

The rider seated himself. "My name is Yount. William Yount." He lifted and turned back the cuff of a coat sleeve to let the silvered surface of a badge shine momentarily in the light.

"Glad to know you," responded the sheriff, interest focusing. "What can I do?"

"I am looking for a man."

"Good place to come. The hills out yonder are full of men somebody's lookin' for — all bashful. A rough section."

"So I've heard," acquiesced Yount. "Which is one reason I came this way. Who's your chief outlaw roundabout?"

"Tonto Bill," said the sheriff promptly. "But if it's him you want, that's a hard number. Tonto don't take easy."

"Not sure he's the man," explained Yount. "The question was mostly asked out of curiosity. My quest is a sort of blind one." Then: "I've heard you were on the level. Otherwise I would not be impartin' this information."

The sheriff took up a pencil and casually ran the point across the top of his desk. "I do what I can. This county wants its law officer to have a quick hand, but a light one. I try to keep a balance, nothin' much more. Public opinion frowns on an uneven deal and violence too close to home. Outside of that, live and let live is our motto. However, if you've got a warrant for Tonto and you insist on havin' him I'll try to get the gent."

"May be him, may not be," mused Yount, observing an item of interest concerning the sheriff. McLean's gun was strapped to his left side, indicating he went into action from that quarter. But he held and used his pencil with the right hand. Yount, whose whole life had been spent in gathering such odd fragments of fact, stored the knowledge away in his mind, drawling on: "I carry a warrant which is four years old."

McLean straightened to attention. The pencil came to a halt. "Long time ago," he murmured. "Who's it for — and what for?"

"There used to be a gang operating around the Crooked River country at that time. A hard, wild bunch. We've cleaned 'em out through the years, all but one. We heard he skipped north — also around four years ago and right after a train holdup which was the gang's last job. His capture has sort of hung fire. Our office has had a lot of other things to do. But recently the railroad company got on our necks. It's a matter of record and precedent with the company. It wants this man — money and time regardless. His name is Orlo Brant — or was in them days when he helped hold up the train."

"Ever see him?"

"Not me. All I have's a description. Five feet eleven; gray eyes; weighs about one hundred-sixty; black hair."

"It might be anybody," said the sheriff. "Nine men out of ten carry black hair here. A good half will run to that height and weight. As for gray eyes, you can pick 'em off the bushes. It might be Tonto, it might be Lost Eagle's banker. Or it might be me."

Yount added, quietly: "And he carries a nipplin' gunshot scar at the right elbow."

The sheriff turned to the girl. She slipped from the packing box and climbed into his lap. He laid a fold of his coat around her slim shoulders. "Don't you catch cold, honey. Well, Yount, how would you tell? Folks don't roll back their sleeves much."

"True. It's a slim trail."

The sheriff ran his hand across the girl's dark hair. He seemed drifting in a channel of thought from which it was difficult to withdraw. "Can't be of much help to you. But the records of this office are at your disposal. So is my influence, such as it is; not much help, I guess."

"Thanks," said Yount. "I'll be around for a spell. Nothing definite. But I'm a great hand to drift and let things happen. In the course of a fairly long life I have observed folks usually give themselves away. You can't hide a thing forever. The more you try, the sooner it creeps out. Time's a powerful chemical thataway."

"Just so," muttered the sheriff, frowning. "Always comes a time to pay the bill. Did that bunch make a good haul off the train?"

"Not a dime. There was six. Two died on the spot, shot to ribbons. The rest broke clear — which was where this Orlo Brant got the bullet in his elbow. They're all jailed now or dead, except him."

Deep lines appeared on the sheriff's broad forehead. His arms tightened about the girl, who solemnly looked up. "Lucky for the gent," he said. "Or maybe unlucky, considerin' what must be on his mind. Four years is a stretch of time, and railroads don't forget."

"Correct." Yount leaned forward. His face, which was normally rather cold and watchful, kindled with kindliness. "Honey, what might be your name?"

"Linnie Marie."

"Think of that! Fits you, too. How old are you, Linnie Marie?"

She paused. The sheriff supplied the answer: "Three years, seven months, two days."

Yount chuckled, a rare thing for him to do. "Got it pat, uh?"

64

"Not an item to be forgotten. You married?"

"I missed that somewhere on the road," said Yount slowly. The sheriff looked down at a sleepy Linnie Marie and mused. "There's a difference."

Yount rose and went to the door. "See you tomorrow." The sheriff nodded.

Yount walked down to the porch of the town's hotel and paused there to finish the end of his cigar. He made no attempt to shelter himself, but the pooling shadows hid him effectively and thus he presently observed the sheriff come from the office and pass by, carrying Linnie Marie in his broad arms; the man seemed to look far ahead, to be plunged in somber reflection. Something in the scene stirred Yount and the tip of his cigar glowed brightly. Then, tossing away the shredded butt, he went in, signed for a room and mounted the creaking stairs.

The room was like a thousand others in which he had spent the active years of his life — musty, shabby, and bearing the scars of many others who had tarried but briefly. Sitting on the edge of the bed, Yount pulled off a boot and held it in his hand. The direct eyes narrowed from the impulse of a thought.

"Linnie Marie. Three years, seven months, two days. He had it pat. Now that's odd. A man's no hand to recollect such a thing. Not unless it's planted in his memory awful strong. Not unless it means more to him than anything else in his life."

In the morning, rising late, Yount crossed to the restaurant and sat up to the counter for his customary coffee and doughnuts. The place was empty except for a comely young waitress and a red-haired rider who instantly ceased talking to her and moved toward the rear of the room.

The girl served Yount and retreated. Yount heard her say: "Well, you can leave for a while, can't you?"

"No. Listen, I've got to make a stand somewhere."

"And be killed? Oh, Jim!"

"Shush."

Yount's gaze was fixed on the counter. He finished his coffee, lit a cigar and contemplated the wreathing smoke. The girl murmured:

"That's pride!"

"Self-respect. Can't run forever."

"But what about me!"

Yount let a long, studious glance fall upon the pair — a tall, frank young man resisting the persuasive talk of a girl made miserable by fear. Then he paid for his breakfast and went back to the hotel where he took a seat on the porch.

Bright sunlight flooded Lost Eagle and under the impetus of the crisp air life ran energetically. Riders posted in, a freighter rolled past. Off toward the outskirts of the town a pall of dust billowed up thickly from a driven herd; on the northern sky line lay rolling hills.

The sheriff strolled up and sat on the steps. "Anything I can do for you, Yount?"

"Just soakin' in the air."

"Good idea," said the sheriff. "There's a time for everything."

In the clearer light of morning, Yount's first impressions of the sheriff were strengthened. The latter's shoulders were muscular, his frame raw-boned. Kindliness rested in the gray, even eyes. About him was a sense of awkward, honest power. When he rolled a cigarette, no deftness in his fingers, the arch of his eyebrows sharpened in concentration and when he spoke there was a trailing drawl in the words:

"Was tryin' to figure why you thought Tonto was your man."

"Maybe he ain't," said Yount. "But I'd heard about him, so thought I'd like to see his face. We get the dope on these fellows down at the main office. This Orlo Brant wasn't a fool. He had brains. He got clear of the bad crowd and stayed clear. He's above average and he'd be the kind to run his own spread. Like Tonto."

"Just so — if he was still on the dodge," mused the sheriff. After a considerable silence he added, "But supposin' he might have turned honest?"

"If so, he probably amounts to somethin' in his community. His kind wouldn't play second fiddle anywhere."

The sheriff studied his own big hands. "Yeah. But bein' honest won't help him now. A man has to pay his bills and those kind of bills never die."

"Correct," agreed Yount.

McLean rose. "It goes against the grain sometimes — this catchin' men who have made mistakes and are tryin' to start again. I've had to do it. It hurts."

Yount's voice was hard. "A man wearing the star can't let sentiment sway him. If the business hurts, he had ought to turn the star in. Man-huntin's a sorry game, often a bitter one."

The red-head came from the restaurant and walked in the direction of the saloon. Yount indicated him with a nod of the head. "Who's that?"

"Jim Lane. With possibilities — if let alone."

Yount watched the sheriff go down the street and intercept the red-head. He saw him put an arm on the young man's shoulder, saw the two, talking earnestly, pass by the saloon. Yount's eyes registered approval. "Slick way of easin' the kid away from drink. McLean's got a heart. Situation here I don't seem to make. Somebody's sittin' on a keg of powder."

For some moments his attention had rested on a faded sign across the way: Lord County Bugle. Rising, he casually crossed the street and stepped into the unkempt, dingy ante-room of a cowtown weekly. A press ceased clacking in the back shop and a man with ink-stained fingers came forward. Yount bowed politely.

"Like to look over your old files if there is no objection."

The printer-publisher nodded to a book-case and retreated. Yount went over, selected a volume whose date was four years old, and carried it to the counter. Extracting a pair of steel-rimmed glasses from his pocket, he adjusted them and proceeded to read. Considerably well along in the yellowed pages his traveling finger stopped on this brief note:

"Cliff McLean and wife, from Dakota Territory, have come to settle in our town. They have rented Nate Splawn's house. Welcome, Cliff, you'll like the climate."

69

"Arriving here in March," said Yount to himself, noting the date. A very few pages farther the McLeans were again mentioned:

"Comes to Mr. and Mrs. Cliff McLean a girl, seven pounds on the store scales which were taken down to register that important event. Linnie Marie is the name of this bouncing little lady, and she looks just like her parents, who are mighty popular people. We suspect Cliff wanted a male heir to pump the bellows at his blacksmith shop — bought from Cal Kelvy — but he bears the disappointment well. The cigar was fine, Cliff."

Yount removed his glasses, rubbed them vigorously. "From Dakota Territory. Not quite four years ago. A good place to give as an address — if a man wanted to be vague about his past. It's a long way off."

He went on with his reading, changing volumes. Occasionally the McLean family was chronicled in homely little items of interest only to a settlement hungry for personal news. Linnie Marie had been sick. Linnie Marie was better. The McLean family had bought Nate Splawn's house. Cliff had sent for a French horn and joined the band. Mention of Cliff as deputy followed; then, the paper announced the election of "that highly popular son of the vicinage as sheriff." Yount suddenly closed the book and replaced it. He had read enough. "Never mentioned him as takin' a trip outside. He's been buried here. Four long years. And never a contact with the rest of the world." Yount let his attention roam along the walls of the shop. Pictures hung askew from ceiling to floor. Of sober, hard-mouthed men staring truculently out into space; of stiff groups, frozen into conscious postures. Yount walked nearer, interest aroused by one such group. It was a cowboy band, mounted and in its full regalia — chaps, gun belts and instruments. The drummer had turned his drum to the camera and upon it was the legend of their organization: "Lost Eagle Bombardeers." In the front rank was Cliff McLean — with his gun hanging at his right side.

Yount's lips came together in a pale, thin line. The printer-newspaper man walked from the rear of the room and stood beside him. "Only cowboy band in this section of the state. Good one, too. Him there, with the horn wrapped around his neck — that's our sheriff. Taken just a short while before he was elected."

"Left-handed man?" asked Yount very softly.

"No-o. Well, for shootin', yes. Some old

accident when he was a kid sorta shortened a muscle in his right arm. So he learned the port-side draw. Don't you forget, he's good enough for most of 'em."

Yount walked from the shop without replying and turned toward the lower end of town, a cold gleam in his eyes. "Orlo Brant — Cliff McLean. One and the same. And may God forgive me, it's him I'm bound to take back to thirty years or life imprisonment for train robbery."

Into the cold whirlwind of thought broke a briskly impersonal voice: "You can walk with me. I'm going to Daddy's."

Yount lifted his head, halting beside a white picket fence. A gravel walk led back to a poplar-shaded house, around which grew banks of hollyhock. In the open gateway stood Linnie Marie, a prim little lady in a starched dress and white shoes. One chubby fist held a bouquet. "Smell," said she, lifting the flowers. "But not too much. Leave some for Daddy."

"Traveling all alone?" asked Yount.

"I'm nearly four," said Linnie Marie, "and practically always have company. There is Mrs. Sanderson's white dog, Nig, who walks as far as the stable. The man with the whiskers takes me across the street. Then I count five doors from the window where the candy is, and that's Daddy's office."

"Allow me," said Yount, offering his hand. Linnie Marie took hold of one finger with a grip that was warm, tight and confident. Her feet made a swift tattoo on the board walk and her black hair glistened in the hot sun. At the next house a solemn mongrel trotted from the shade and sniffed Yount's boots. Linnie Marie tipped her oval face and said:

"He's a *very* 'sponsible dog."

"I don't doubt he'd tear me to pieces if he didn't know I was a friend of yours," agreed Yount, and was filled with a queer, painful sadness. In the deep, unclouded eyes of Linnie Marie there was no hint of either fear or questioning. The world to her was all that it seemed — kindly, smiling, without hurt. And the man, whose life had been wholly spent in a world that was far from kindly, suddenly wondered why things could not be to all men as they were to Linnie Marie at almost four. They had reached the stable and were crossing the street. Cliff McLean swung through a store door and smiled.

"Both of you in pretty good company," he drawled.

Linnie Marie released her grip on Yount's finger and looked up. "Thank you *very* much."

"I wish," began Yount, and was interrupted. Both he and McLean swung to face a giant of a man who came racking into town from the east. He whirled his horse beside the saloon rack, dismounted and passed into the establishment with a swift, hostile side glance at the sheriff.

McLean's features stiffened. "Buck Rose," he muttered. "Bad one but slow. Tonto uses him for a chore boy. Something's in the wind."

"Much trouble with that gang?"

The sheriff considered the question, as if wishing to strike a fair balance. "Well, it won't do to say I'm afraid of the bunch. Only, I'm supposed to leave 'em alone till they get too rough. The county expects me to keep a light rein. We're on the outskirts of law, you know. Beyond the pass is outlaw country, by unanimous agreement. We're content to let it be so as long as they don't overstep their bounds."

"Practical," approved Yount. "Better to isolate a disease than scatter it."

"Yeah," the sheriff muttered. "Only when I see —"

Sudden clamor arose from the saloon. On common impulse both men stepped clear, guiding Linnie Marie with them. The doors swung wide with the pressure of Buck Rose's teetering body. He came backward, both enormous arms beating air and a dumb perplexity

74

showing on his dark face. Before the doors could swing inward, Jim Lane ran through, struck the big man with a pair of solid stomach blows, and sprang clear.

"I'll break yore cursed neck!" boomed Rose.

A bystander came up at the sheriff's beck and carried Linnie Marie away. "It won't do," grunted the sheriff. "God knows she'll learn about misery and trouble soon enough."

"Don't come around here tellin' me what to do, Rose!" cried the red-head. "I'm sick of it! I'm not takin' no orders from Tonto and I ain't trailin' with him, see? I'm through!"

"I'll break yore cursed neck!" repeated Rose and swung his arm as if it were a length of cordwood. The red-head ducked slightly, and Rose, missing his target, was carried off balance. While the giant struggled to recover, the red-head struck. The blow landed, rolling the giant's head skyward until he stared at the sun with a swollen regard. Then, like some maul-struck steer, the big man dropped and rolled in the dust. The red-head spoke between gusts of breathing:

"Go tell Tonto I'm tired of bein' hounded! I want to be let alone!"

Buck Rose crawled to his feet, dust chalking his sweat-mottled face. He gestured toward his gun but the young man's metallic warning halted the motion. "Don't try it! I can beat you to hell any day in the week!"

"Do as yore told or take the consequences!"

"I'll stay right here! Even Tonto can't boost me beyond my limit!"

"We'll be back in an hour to see about that," grumbled Rose, reaching for his saddle. He was seated and preparing to ride away when the sheriff spoke:

"Rose, tell Tonto not to carry the matter any farther."

"Who in hell are you to give orders?" jeered Rose.

"Never mind," countered the sheriff evenly. "I won't have Jim Lane badgered."

"We'll be back in an hour," was Rose's sullen answer; and he rode off.

The sheriff said, "Jim, come to my office now," and turned on his heels. Yount followed them casually. When he reached the sheriff's door he overheard the red-head muttering wearily:

"It's got on my nerves. Maybe I have made some bad blunders. I ain't a saint. But I got wise and left his damn' gang when I saw what the end of the trail would be. I ain't his kind of a crook. I don't think I'd make any kind of a good crook. Now he wants me back. It ain't the first time he's tried. And you can bet he'll be here if he says so."

"Plenty of trails out of town," said the sheriff. But Jim Lane had turned stubborn. "He'd like to see me run. I won't."

The sheriff did not answer. His right arm lay on the desk, crooked at an angle. Time dragged. Presently he spoke: "You want to go straight? You mean that, Jim?"

"I've said it, Sheriff. There's reasons —"

"I know," interrupted the sheriff, and squared his shoulders. Yount, ever observing the man's face, saw signs of a dogged resistance there. "All right. You'll get your chance. Go to the saloon and stay there."

"Listen, Sheriff. This is my quarrel."

McLean brushed that aside impatiently. "I told you what to do. Don't lift your gun, do you hear! Get into the saloon. Nobody can accuse you of being afraid. That's where Tonto will expect to find you and that's where you'll be. But he won't cross the door sill."

"I don't like it."

The sheriff threw up his head. "Damn you, obey my orders!"

Jim Lane, resentful, on the edge of rebellion, stared at the older man. But the sheriff's level glance held him silent, and, nodding curtly, he left. Yount, who had come in and seated himself quietly, smoked his cigar with a kind of aloof detachment.

"Tonto's gone too far," muttered the sheriff, half to himself. "I'll stand for a lot of things but not that. Nothin' in all this universe is so mean as tryin' to keep a man crooked when he wants to be different. Jim's made his mistake and he'll regret it in his conscience the rest of his life. But he's got a chance comin' and I'll see he gets it, by God, if I have to go down in dust!"

"My sentiments," said Yount, laconically. "Need help?"

"Obliged, but I'm expected to handle my own showdowns."

Yount moved toward the door. As an apparent after-thought he added: "I should not presume to interfere, but I'll be somewhere around during the play." Going to the porch he sat down. Men tramped across the porch behind him and he heard the backlash of their comment:

"Cliff's a fool to make an issue of it. Who the hell is Jim Lane that he sh'd drag Cliff into this?"

"Had to be, soon or late."

"Disagree. Tonto's been lettin' him alone, ain't he? Cliff's a good shot but he can't cut it against Tonto. Not with a left-hand draw that's only three years old. It won't work. He'll get himself killed. Dammit, it ain't right!"

Yount rose and went to his room. It was stifling hot. He removed his coat and tramped the floor, halting once to drink tepid water from the pitcher; staring through the window at the glittering hills.

"He made a mistake. Never in a hundred years should he have run for sheriff. It lifted him up to public observation. He should have played the humble part all the way through. But he's a better-than-average man and couldn't stay down. Some kind of a law governin' these things. God only knows what kind of a law stands behind what I've got to do."

Time dragged. Through the open window came the groan of a passing flat-bed wagon; after which came an intensified, expectant silence. "Better for him to die in a fight with this Tonto. No disgrace to his wife or the little girl. Nothing but an empty place in the house."

The thought brought him to a standstill. An empty place. There was something inexpressibly sad about the idea. He knew the meaning of emptiness, of going along a lonely trail. . . .

Outside a solitary rider's approach echoed flatly, breaking into Yount's grim reverie. He put on his coat, drew his gun and let it lie in one palm. Slipping the catch, he spun the cylinder thoughtfully, snapped it home, dropped the gun lightly into its holster. Turning out, he caught sight of himself in the clouded mirror of the washstand and was shocked into momentary quiescence. All that his life was, stared relentlessly back. The discipline of service was engraved in every lineament, to remind him he had never shirked a disagreeable task, never temporized, never failed to live up to the badge he wore. A cold face looked out at him, a face old and set and humorless. A man-hunter's face. It was as if his conscience rose to remind him of the one inescapable fact: no matter how cruelly his act might cut into the lives of others, he had a duty to perform, a man to account for in the name of that justice he had sworn to uphold.

His last cigar was a shredded wreck. Going to the street, he walked to the drug store to replenish his pockets and, upon entering, found the sheriff and Linnie Marie eating ice cream at a table. Linnie Marie's slim legs dangled from her chair. She waved a spoon to Yount and smiled — a sudden, beaming smile. The sheriff nodded. "Draw up and join us."

"It'll make you fat," said Linnie Marie.

"Honey," cautioned the sheriff, "only monkeys eat thataway. I'll have to build sideboards on the spoon."

"When I'm six," said Linnie Marie, "Daddy's going to get me a piano."

The sheriff looked at Yount almost apologetically. "It ain't as foolish as it sounds. There's an old one at the opera house I can get for a whistle. Linnie's got an ear for music."

"Do you play with ears?" asked Linnie Marie. But she never waited for an answer. Her attention fastened on Yount's massive watch chain.

A man came swiftly into the drug store and beckoned to the sheriff with one significant backward nod of his head. McLean rose, very slowly, very deliberately.

"Put up half a pint of cream to take out," he said to the clerk. "Linnie, I'll be back in a minute. You wait, and we'll go home with a present for Mother." He stepped back a pace, eyes absorbing the picture of Linnie Marie; his hand dropped to her head, brushed it and fell away. Turning, he walked from the store.

Yount rose and followed, stationing himself in a slim lane of shadow made by a porch post. To his right he saw McLean posted in the middle of the street under the full glare of the sun; waiting quietly, head thrown slightly forward and big arms idle. At the other end of town Tonto Bill was coming in, a half-dozen men strung out behind him. A citizen started across the street, was sharply

81

warned and nearly fell in his hurry to retreat. Tonto, riding slowly, reached the saloon and halted. He stepped from the saddle, a catlike figure, swart and hawk-cheeked and with half a grin on his face. Then, seeming to see the sheriff for the first time, he squared himself to face the official. Yount, rolling a dry cigar between his lips, judged a space of twenty feet intervened between the two men. Tonto Bill threw a quick, impatient challenge down that still, light-drenched strip:

"Heard you warned me to stay clear of Lost Eagle. That so?"

The sheriff's reply was a little low: "I told you not to carry this business any farther, Tonto."

"Speak up," jeered the outlaw. "Don't whisper. What made you think I'd obey?"

"Let it ride. You won't interfere with Jim Lane."

"Feelin' yore authority? Don't you know I give orders, not take 'em?"

"In this case you'll take them."

The outlaw yelled: "Supposin' I don't?"

"In that case," said the sheriff, dragging the words out, "I will wait for you to draw."

Tonto swayed. His followers, still mounted, broke ranks and crowded to either walk. Yount, rigidly absorbed, clenched the cigar between his teeth. Somewhere on the extreme corner of his vision was the white strained face of a townsman. Tonto laughed — a harsh, sardonic laugh — then reached for his gun.

A double blast ripped through the silence. Tonto buckled in the middle as if punched there; his arm fell, the gun dropped from trailing fingers and then, obviously fighting to hold in the last coursing impulses of life, he went to his knees and collapsed.

Somebody yelled. Yount stepped from the walk, lifted his gun and set it against the rigid horsemen. Standing there, straight and self-contained, and with his cold glance slicing across the distance, he spoke:

"My name is William Yount. I speak as a ranger of this state. Carry this business any farther and I shall see you all caught and hanged."

The renegade group, numbed by the death of a man they had believed unbeatable, were caught beyond the chance of a draw. The redhead charged from the saloon, ready to fire. Some stiff-backed citizen ran out of a store, shotgun poked forward. The sheriff, who had never stirred from his tracks, spoke:

"If a man wants to go straight in my town he will have the chance to do it. Get back to the hills!"

The horsemen wheeled without ceremony and rode off. A tide of resuming life flowed through the street. Tonto's body was surrounded and blocked from sight.

The sheriff ran into the drug store and reappeared with Linnie Marie in his arms, shielding her face from the crowd and the dead man. Yount replaced his gun, looked at his bitten cigar and threw it to the dust. The hotel man came by, breathing hard. Yount handed him a dollar. "My bill," said he, and walked directly to the stable. "Saddle up for me." Crossing the street, he entered the sheriff's office.

McLean sat in a chair with Linnie Marie cradled in his lap, both broad palms protectively around her. His eyes were on the door and when he discovered Yount advancing, a look of pain spread over his patient face.

"I've come to say good-by," said Yount.

The sheriff flinched. "How —"

"I'm returnin' to headquarters. My report is that Orlo Brant died in the street of Lost Eagle with a bullet in his heart. The record is closed, sir."

The sheriff put Linnie Marie to the floor and stood up. He appeared to be holding himself together with an effort. "Tonto —"

"Who can be sure?" broke in Yount, as if not wishing to hear more. "The record is closed."

"Yount — you're a white man!"

"Pretty hard to bury a secret deep enough to keen it from showin'," mused Yount. He seemed to want to say more, but checked the impulse and looked to a grave Linnie Marie who stood back watching, not understanding the brief phrases running over her head yet somehow feeling the undercurrent of a situation outside the bright, smooth channel of her day. Yount bent and lifted her.

"Linnie Marie," said he, music coming to the cold drawl, "in just a little while you'll be four. When you light those candles, remember one of them stands for an old fellow a long ways off down a lonesome trail. Just think of me once before you go to bed that night."

"You want a kiss?" asked Linnie Marie. "Aw'right." And her small arms went about his neck, while her kiss was quick and generous. Yount set her down; he inclined his head to the sheriff, gruffly formal:

"Pleasure to have met you. Three years, seven months, two days. You bet it makes a difference. . . . Well, good-by."

He turned and went to his horse. Mounted, he rode slowly from Lost Eagle in the blaze of a high, hot sun — a stiff and sure man looking straight ahead into that long, long distance beyond the heat haze. At the edge of town he turned to see Linnie Marie standing in the street, one small hand lifted for a last farewell. Yount removed his hat and bowed as he would have bowed to the finest lady of the land and pressed on, alone.

The Colonel's Daughter

They had eaten in the sultry heat of the house and were now on the porch to catch the evening's first breath of air, with the colored light of the hanging Chinese lanterns shining pleasantly down, and the gentlemen smoking the colonel's cigars. The guests were Major and Mrs. Grant, Captain Keil of A Troop and his wife, Lieutenant Reading with his Baltimore bride of six months, Doctor Jury, and Lieutenants Cavour Watkins and Jeff Lee. And Taisie Belknap — for the colonel had a daughter.

This was at old Fort Tonto in the summer of a year the Apaches were particularly bad. The boots of the guard relief sharply struck the iron-hard parade ground in passing by and the challenge of post number three was a drowsy, taciturn murmur as the relief reached it. The blackness of this night was very deep, and further thickened by the shadow of Mesquite Mountain hovering over the post; and above was the ageless, cloudy glitter of stars.

The colonel's wife said; "Well, suppose we

have the masquerade party on Saturday night. That will give us time to invite our friends down from Prescott."

"I shall come disguised as a scarecrow," asserted Lieutenant Reading's young bride in a tone of sulky discontent. "It will require so little alteration in the way I look, or feel." She was new to the Army ways and hadn't forgotten Baltimore yet. The colonel's wife was gently amused. "I recall the same despair thirty-seven years ago."

Captain Keil's wife added: "When you have worn your best dress for five years, you will no longer mind it."

The major's wife said: "I have not left the frontier since 1869." And silence came on them, for everybody understood how bitter the major's wife was from knowing her husband would never reach a higher rank.

Taisie Belknap swayed in a rocker whose motion rhythmically racked the heat-warped floor boards. Her blond head lay comfortably tilted and her legs were stretched out in a manner that would have been improper in Baltimore. Taisie had been born in an Army ambulance five miles behind the battle of Bull Run, cradled in trunk lids through babyhood. She was a thorough Army girl, now definitely arrived at a tawny, silent and graceful beauty.

The colonel was speaking in a husky, idle

voice of the Custer campaign of '76; and
Taisie, silent and in the shadows, could see
how his talk affected Cavour Watkins, and
seemed not to affect Jeff Lee. There was this
deep difference in them that pulled strongly
at her interest. Cavour Watkins listened with
his ears and his eyes and his heart. She could
see him respond to those old battles; she could
see how his imagination fired up. He was a
stocky shape in the shadows, blackened by
the sun and shaped like the traditional cavalryman. A man, she thought, made to ride and
to fight — and to love action because of the
vitality in him. Jeff Lee sat low in his chair,
his tall shape angularly slouched and his sorrel
head tipped a little. He was lost in his thoughts
and his broad mouth made a straight, reflec-
tive line across an inscrutable face; and Taisie
doubted if he heard her father's words at all.

The post's challenge curtly lifted and carried along the still air, and a horseman
pounded up the parade, wheeling at the
colonel's porch, his presence bringing all the
officers to their feet. The rider jumped down
and Taisie saw the pallid dust mask coating
his face. He was hard put for breath.

"They raided Wilton's ranch an hour ago.
Wilton and Wilton's wife are dead. They
burned everything but the shed me and the
boys was in. It was Tobeel's band again, about

ten in the bunch."

"Which way did they go?"

"Back toward the Mesquites."

The colonel was a round, jolly man who concealed his excellence behind a disarming blandness. He said: "You've had a hard ride, Jack. Get some coffee from the mess shack." He stood there, quietly considering, while ease went away from the porch. A sergeant ran up and halted at the porch.

The colonel said: "Lieutenant Watkins, take twenty men and follow the trail. But don't go beyond the Lordsburg Pass. Take Reading along."

The sergeant at the foot of the porch wheeled into the darkness immediately. Cavour Watkins made his bow to the party and looked across at Taisie Belknap. He was smiling and he was pleased as he went away with young Reading, the civilian wearily following. Over by B Troop's quarters was the sergeant's leather voice calling. Lights began to swing around the picket line.

Taisie watched worry stiffen Jeff Lee's cheeks. He faced the colonel and said, "With your permission, sir," bowed and dropped into outer darkness rapidly. Captain Keil drawled: "Jeff's worried about his domesticated Injuns."

"I share the worry," murmured the colonel.

90

"There are no domesticated Apaches," said Major Grant. He rendered his stiff compliments and took his wife's arm. The Keils left, and the doctor escorted Reading's wife toward her quarters.

"Taisie," said the colonel's wife, "I really wish you'd sit in that chair instead of lying in it like Jeff Lee does. Some day you'll break your neck."

Taisie smiled and said, "I must remember Mrs. Chaffee's Seminary," and vanished into the darkness. Cavour Watkins' detail counted fours on the parade, those voices blunt and heavy in the night. Lanterns flashed brilliantly along the picket line.

The colonel's wife said: "I wish she weren't so pretty and I wish she'd make up her mind. At her age I was married two years."

The colonel pulled at the trailing edges of his mustache; the light of the lanterns deepened the florid color of his cheeks. "She's made up her mind."

"Which one?"

"Don't know. Neither does she. But it will be one of them."

The colonel's wife said: "You have a preference?"

But the colonel was an impartial man, even in front of his wife. "Both excellent officers. Watkins is a born Indian fighter. Cuts a dash, after the Phil Sheridan style. Enormously ambitious."

She said: "I think Jeff Lee feels it when you keep him behind so much. He hasn't been on a scout this year."

"Serves his purpose," said the colonel briefly, and stood on the porch to watch the shadows of Cavour Watkins' detail form up.

Taisie stood by the guardhouse wall. Cavour Watkins came from his quarters and stopped a moment there. He said: "I'll see you —" and waited until the noise of counting off was done before going on. "I'll see you tomorrow afternoon."

She said: "Be careful, Cavour."

He was laughing.

"Taisie — I'd like your glove to tie on my belt. A token."

"A very gallant thought, Cavour. Be careful."

"You worry for me?"

Her voice was soft and cool. "I love all those rawboned old Irishmen."

"But as for me?" said Cavour Watkins.

Her tone was quick and gay and gently mocking. "It takes fifteen years to make a good sergeant, Cavour, and only four to turn out a lieutenant."

"Good lieutenants," he said, "are born, not made." And went toward his detail. She remained by the guardhouse wall, under the glow of the fixed lantern, hearing Cavour's command. The detail trotted by, fell into the desert road and at last faded, the clatter of saddle furniture dying in the deep silence.

Out there a quarter mile the fires of Kaminzin's peaceful Apache band burned orange holes against the night. Jeff Lee would be down there, calming Kaminzin's fears. Tobeel and half of the Apaches in this district stuck to the Mesquites and raided the white settlements. The other half, under Kaminzin, had made peace and were camped along Santa Rita Creek. Yet even in peace Kaminzin's people were wild as antelopes and subject to fright. The least whisper would set them in flight for the hills again and spoil her father's work. General Crook's orders were plain: peace to those who would come in, destruction to those who would not. Cavour Watkins was on his way to destroy while Jeff Lee crouched before a fire in Kaminzin's camp and talked their tongue, patient and careful and kindly; shrewdly matching his words to their primitive emotions.

She walked back along officers' row.

The post challenged and she heard Jeff Lee's answer as he came up from the Indian camp. His shoulders made a broad, square shape against the dark, but she could tell by the swing of his body that he was tired.

She said: "What was wrong with Kaminzin?"

He stood beside her, packing his pipe.

"One of Tobeel's men slipped into the camp and got to telling Kaminzin's people we would turn the troops loose on them some night and kill them all. Kaminzin trusts me, but it's hard for him to keep his camp from getting scary. Tobeel's trying to get them to run for the hills and start fighting again."

"What did you tell them?"

He said laconically: "Just sat and talked. It's ticklish. The wrong word and they'd all run for the Mesquites, which would be the end of our work."

The light from his tent touched her briefly and she knew that he was strongly aware of her presence here.

He said: "It has been hot."

Her laughter was a small silver echo through the dark. "How should I answer that, Jeff?"

"Someday," he said briefly, "I may get a tour of service at a post where light conversation is taught dumb officers."

It was a faint flame of anger unexpectedly leaping out of this man's broad and patient surface. It startled her. He stood straight and strange before her, and there was a breath of violence between them. She murmured, "Jeff,

94

I wasn't making fun of you," and put a hand on his arm.

"No," he said flatly. "I'm sorry. Good night, Taisie."

In her room she undressed and threw a robe around her and stood thoughtfully still. The long, dreaming notes of taps turned her out to her cot on officers' row; and lying there with the universe arched above, she thought of the strangeness of men. Jeff Lee saw nothing in the night or in her to lift him. Cavour Watkins would have walked with her across the parade, challenged and turned a little reckless.

At eight o'clock Taisie stepped into her sidesaddle for the morning's ride. She returned, and, changed out of her riding clothes, sat on the porch to reread her letters from the East, all of them a month old.

After lunch, still on the porch, she settled to her needlework, quelling a quick rebellion at the chore.

Around four o'clock three old Indians stalked up from Kaminzin's camp and halted by headquarters. Jeff came out of headquarters and listened motionlessly and walked back with them toward the camp on the Santa Rita. Colonel Belknap strolled up the walk and sat down beside Taisie on the porch, his round cheeks a violent red.

Taisie bowed her head carefully over the sewing. Her talk came out very casually. "Jeff seems to have influence over Kaminzin's people."

Belknap said, "Yes," briefly.

"More than Cavour?"

"Different type of man." And added instantly, "Both good officers." There was that impartiality she could not break through, even though she knew he had his own secret preference. The frontier showed up weakness and it showed up strength — and men out here were both just and cruel in their appraisal of other men. Her father said nothing, yet it was Cavour Watkins whom he invariably sent on scout while Jeff Lee sweated out his ambition on the detailed drudgery at the post.

"I have wondered why you never send Jeff Lee into the Mesquites!"

"Useful to me here," answered the colonel and then stood up. There was the scuffle of hoofs on the flinty trail on the hill above camp; and looking that way Taisie saw Cavour Watkins' detail file slowly down into the post. Belknap said in a deeply relieved way: "Time they were back," and went to the steps.

Exhaustion rode that detail, bowing each man over in the saddle. Cavour Watkins stepped to the ground and made his salute to the colonel. His eyes, bloodshot, showed the flicker of fire. He said: "Reporting back with the detail, sir. We had a brush with Tobeel near the gates of Lordsburg Pass about daylight, but he got away. On our return we surprised a rancheria and broke it up. I regret to report the loss of Private Hannevy."

Taisie Belknap's glance rushed down the column and found a horse bearing a blanketed burden lashed across its saddle. Her father's voice was even and unrevealing. "Very good, Lieutenant," and he stood there until Cavour Watkins saluted and mounted and took his detail down to the barracks. The colonel's hand pulled at the ends of his mustache and the florid color deepened and Taisie knew he was strongly stirred. Jeff Lee was coming up from Kaminzin's camp; he turned at the guardhouse and stood observing Watkins' detail climb stiffly out of saddle, and afterward Taisie saw him wheel without speaking to Cavour Watkins and go to his quarters.

At six-thirty they ate in the trapped heat of the dining room, without appetite and without much talk. When the colonel lost a man his jolliness went away. At seven Taisie walked into the kitchen to have a word with Charley Simpson, who had been their enlisted cook for ten years. Charley was a close-mouthed man inclined to taciturnity but all the gossip of the post came to him as iron filings drift to a magnet, which Taisie knew. She said:

"What happened, Charley?"

Charley rested his hands on the edge of the washpan. "Sergeant Riley says they didn't rest more than twenty minutes all night. They caught up with Tobeel and had a brush up by the pass, but the 'Paches were firing out of the rocks and the lieutenant tried a charge, which is where he lost Hannevy. Tobeel slipped away and the horses were too done up to make a chase. Comin' back they scouted the rock breaks along the crest of the hills and surprised a rancheria. There was six bucks and some women and a couple kids. They made a fight but the lieutenant broke 'em up. One of the squaws shot Sergeant Riley through the arm." Taisie murmured: "The women and children, Simpson — what happened to them?"

Simpson looked into the washpan's suds. He said in a noncommittal voice: "I didn't hear. Got away, I guess."

Taisie knew he was lying. Some of those women had been killed in the thick of the fight. She went out, thinking of that, and walked the parade with her yellow head down and her leggy body swinging. The sun dropped over the western line and when she had climbed the trail to number eight sentry post on the bluff of the hill she saw the purple waves of dusk rolling across the far desert. Lights began to glitter through the post windows and it was full dark when she returned; and all the officers of the post were on the colonel's porch.

Cavour Watkins had changed into a fresh uniform and when he stood up she noticed how solid and aggressive a shape he made, how stout his pride was. He was smiling at her and she could tell that the ambition in him had been fanned and strengthened by the day's work. Jeff Lee came to his feet with a brief politeness and sat down again, slouching disjointedly in his chair.

Cavour Watkins said: "I am convinced that Jeff's peaceful Indians are betraying us. I believe Kaminzin sends messengers to Tobeel as soon as our details leave the fort."

Jeff Lee said from the depths of his chair: "Kaminzin an honest man."

Cavour Watkins grinned. "I cannot be so naïve. They all hate us and bide their time to get even. Nothing will ever pacify them, except gunfire."

"Tobeel fights because he believes he will be killed if he surrenders," said Jeff Lee. "I cannot blame his reasoning altogether. Kaminzin has surrendered because he trusts our word. If we keep our word with him, he'll gradually persuade most of Tobeel's fighters to come in and give up."

Cavour Watkins said impatiently: "They accept our rations and laugh at us."

Behind those two voices Taisie heard a difference that nothing could reconcile; the oppositeness of two men who could never in a whole lifetime agree. Somebody spoke in Apache at the corner of the porch, surprising them all. Three of Kaminzin's band had come soundlessly across the parade and made faint shapes in the gathered dusk. Jeff Lee rose and was across the porch immediately, all his indifference was gone; and he stood before these three shadows and talked a while, the exchange of Apache talk quick and harsh. Presently they went away as silently as they had come.

Jeff Lee had changed again, anger pulling his long lips together and lighting a fire in his eyes. "Kaminzin's people are uneasy. They're afraid something's going to happen to them because Private Hannevy was killed."

Colonel Belknap said: "Who started that?"

Silence flowed the porch significantly. Jeff Lee stood tall and heavy-shouldered against the lamplight. Cavour Watkins watched Jeff Lee with a bright and narrow interest, as though he listened for some particular thing to be said. Taisie saw this, but Jeff Lee drawled: "I don't know, sir," and left the porch. Cavour Watkins rose promptly and the other officers paid their respects and walked away.

At taps Taisie went into her room, undressed for bed and slipped on her robe, hearing the murmur of her folks beyond the wall; and went out to the cot on the line. For a while she lay there watching the sweep of the sky, remembering that in another month she would be twenty-three years old. That was old, so very old. . . .

The sound of voices over by the porch wakened her suddenly. A lantern flashed there and she saw the officers of the post gathered by her father, who stood in his white nightgown and bare feet, with his nightcap sagged on his head like a cornucopia.

Jeff Lee was saying: "They left camp without a sound, Kaminzin and his whole band. It must have been around taps, but nobody on the guardhouse post saw them or heard them go."

"That's Apaches for you," grumbled Major Grant. "Two hundred getting away without raising an echo. They'll be up in the Mesquites before daylight."

"Raiding the Santa Rita valley before dark," added Cavour Watkins. "It was clever of Kaminzin to fatten his warriors on our rations before starting the fall raids. There are no honest Apaches, Lieutenant Lee. You have been fooled."

Jeff Lee said evenly: "I do not think I have. I know Kaminzin. If the colonel will give me permission to take Sergeant Oldroyd I'll have Kaminzin back by noon."

Colonel Belknap said slowly: "You are that confident, Lieutenant Lee?"

"I know Kaminzin's people. They're afraid, because Hannevy's dead. They expect trouble from us, which is what they were threatened with."

Taisie watched her father with wonder. He stood in his bare feet and looked steadily at Jeff Lee, whom he had always kept behind for routine chores, and said: "You have my permission. . . ."

After breakfast Taisie walked into the kitchen to talk to Charley Simpson.

She said: "What scared Kaminzin, Charley?"

Simpson diced a potato carefully on his cutting board. "I heard that somebody went down there before dinner last night and told Kaminzin he'd better help get Tobeel or there'd be trouble."

"Who went down there, Charley?"

Charley Simpson said gently: "Don't believe I heard."

102

At eleven o'clock she went down to the mess hall and stood in a corner while the doctor said a few words over Hannevy's coffin. Six enlisted men lifted the coffin out to an army wagon and A and B troops walked in formation across the parade to the cemetery at the edge of Santa Rita Creek. The colonel's regimental band was back at brigade headquarters in Omaha but four Irishmen came from the ranks and sang a hymn and the doctor made his prayer and a squad fired to the sky as they lowered Hannevy; and then Taisie looked up from the earth to the stony sides of the hill and saw Kaminzin's band file down that slope two and two, with the blue figures of Jeff Lee and Sergeant Oldroyd in the lead.

She saw all the faces of the assembled Irish troopers swing to the hill, showing relief, even through the burnt, bleak hardness of their features. Her father pulled at the ends of his mustache vigorously and Lieutenant Reading's wife brushed her eyes at one quick gesture. She looked at Cavour Watkins, impelled by a curiosity that she didn't understand; and saw how narrowly he watched that approaching band, his eyes strictly guarded.

It was noon, as Jeff Lee had promised. Later, from the porch, she saw him cross to headquarters, high and broad in the sunlight; and presently he came out with her father and then the post officers assembled and all of them went down past the guardhouse to pay Kaminzin a call. Charley Simpson strode over the parade to B Troop's barracks like an eager hound on scent. Taisie entered the house for her sewing and came back and sat there with a consuming impatience that deepened the color on her cheeks. Action whirled around the parade and left her high and dry. The officers were returning and she saw Cavour Watkins stride off to the stable. The rest of them were talking in front of headquarters and her father shook Jeff Lee's hand, after which Jeff Lee made an abrupt turn, following Cavour Watkins. Taisie's needle dug into the sewing and stopped and her eyes got stormy. She said, "Damn," and saw Charley Simpson come back from B Troop's quarters. She was in the kitchen when Charley reached it.

She said: "From the beginning, Charley. From the beginning."

"Well, the lieutenant and Oldroyd went right into the heart of the Mesquites. Oldroyd said it was dark as pitch and he didn't know where they was. But the lieutenant went like he was in the middle of a straight street. They hit Kaminzin's camp about three in the morning and the lieutenant hollered something ahead in Apache. Somebody shot at them and then Kaminzin stopped it and they rode straight at a little fire. The lieutenant got down and Oldroyd said it looked like every 'Pache in Arizona was there. Tobeel was there, too. And everybody was pretty mad and Tobeel raised his gun on the lieutenant but Kaminzin knocked it aside. The lieutenant got off his horse and the 'Paches grabbed the horse and then all Oldroyd could see was the lieutenant's hair somewhere in the middle of all them Injuns, with everybody boilin' over.

"Oldroyd said the lieutenant didn't move and didn't say a word for ten minutes and then they quit yellin' and Kaminzin and Tobeel and a bunch of little chiefs hunkered up by the fire and began to parley. They talked for two hours and every now and then a squaw would yell and rush at the lieutenant and once in a while Tobeel would get up and make a speech. About daylight, when everything was calmed down, Tobeel stood up again and drew a knife and ran at the lieutenant. And then Kaminzin lifted a gun and killed Tobeel. And just at sunrise Oldroyd said Kaminzin rose off his hunkers and said about six words and the whole camp got on their horses and started back for the Santa Rita. By God, Miss Taisie, that lieutenant is a cool one."

Taisie said softly, "Thank you, Charley," and went back and sat down on the porch.

She put her sewing in her lap and waited, her eyes lifting to the parade and falling and lifting again, her chin turning stubborn.

Jeff Lee came into the half shadows of the stable and found Cavour Watkins sitting on a bale of hay. B Troop's stable sergeant was there, too, but he looked carefully at Cavour Watkins and at Jeff Lee and swung on his heels and went out. Cavour Watkins had risen to his feet, a full and violent shine in his eyes. His talk hit at Jeff Lee with a wicked gustiness.

"My compliments, Lieutenant Lee. It was very dramatic. Very picturesque. You will have splendid notices of this all up and down the frontier."

"Cavour," said Lee, "don't ever go down to Kaminzin again and threaten him."

"Tell Belknap I was the man!" cried Cavour Watkins. "Damn your Indians."

Jeff Lee's face was shadowed and hard with his thoughts. "How far would you go for your personal ambition, Cavour?"

Cavour's eyes were bitter-bright. He took a step forward, smiling in a manner that was rashly ungovernable. He said, "You damned garrison drudge," and threw his fist at Jeff Lee's face.

Jeff Lee was moving on. His arm knocked that arriving fist into his chest and he reached

106

Cavour Watkins with one slamming, sledging blow to the chin. Cavour Watkins dropped on the hard earth and lay there, his wind rasping in and out. Jeff Lee wheeled from the stable and found B Troop's stable sergeant staring indifferently across the parade. Jeff Lee said: "Lieutenant Watkins is a little ill. I think it is the sun. Do you understand?"

"It is a powerful sun, sor," said the sergeant gravely.

Taisie lifted her sewing, seeing Jeff Lee swing over the parade with his long legs biting out the distance. Her father had gone into the bedroom for his afternoon nap and she could hear her mother talking to him.

Jeff Lee said, from the foot of the porch: "It is quite hot again."

Taisie looked up. She said, "Yes, Lieutenant, I think it probably is." But she saw something on his solemn face and caught her breath. He was smiling and he was pleased and he was looking at her as a proper officer ought to look at the comely daughter of a colonel. He had, she understood, been through six months of bitterness and personal torment, eating out his heart on the dismal garrison chores while another man rose above him. But he had come through it, his judgment upheld and his faith returned. She could see all that on his face. "I hear," she murmured, looking down at her sewing, "you had an interesting trip."

His eyes were a powdery gray, and they were laughing at her. "Tattoo is a better time to tell you about that. Out along the hill where there might be a breath of wind."

"It has a pleasant sound," she said; and looked up at him in a straight and unsmiling way, without the least reservation. That time had at last come.

The colonel lay on his bed and the colonel's lady stood by the closed bedroom door. She said: "So, it was Jeff Lee. Are you pleased, Belknap?"

Belknap chuckled. "I am quite satisfied."

The colonel's lady said fretfully: "Then why have you favored Cavour with all the exciting details and kept poor Jeff Lee drudging in the sun?"

"A good man always stands seasoning, which is why I ground Jeff on the wheel," Belknap replied.

Dispatch to the General

General Terry lay at the junction of the Yellowstone and Rosebud with the campfires of his two thousand men burning their yellow-dotted blooms through the dark. The blistering July heat, soaked day-long into the soil, now came out of the soil in steady waves and the smell of dust was everywhere as the sergeant reached Terry's open tent flap and stood by, waiting for the general to finish his hasty writing.

Ned Gervaise, the civilian guide, had also arrived and while the two men waited the general's pleasure they exchanged casual inspections, both aware they would be pretty much in each other's hands during the next few days. Gervaise was a wiry little fellow in a once-black broadcloth suit turned green from the rigors of the campaign. He had a goatee, a big nose and a pair of beady, restless eyes and he was supposed to be the best guide in the country, next to Charley Reynolds. But Charley had been massacred five days before and so the sergeant supposed that now made Ned Gervaise the best guide.

General Terry finished his note, sealed it and rose from the table. He gave it to the sergeant. Then the general said, "Sergeant Hounds, you will deliver that dispatch to General Crook, who is somewhere between Fort Fetterman and this point."

"Yes, sir," said the sergeant.

"You may get separated," reflected Terry. "Therefore I had better tell Gervaise the contents of the dispatch in case he alone gets through. General Crook and I were to have met on the Powder River two weeks ago. He has apparently been delayed, and I have been delayed. Tell the general to swing over to the Rosebud and march along it. I am starting out in the morning and will meet him somewhere on the Rosebud. You may tell him the reason for my delay. There are five thousand Sioux and Cheyenne between his command and mine. Tell him to use caution — but to push along."

Gervaise nodded, whereupon the general said, "Have you picked the best possible horses?"

"No horses," said Gervaise. "You can't hide a horse — and we'll be doin' considerable hidin'. I can walk forty miles a night if the sergeant ain't slow."

The sergeant was a tall, willowy lad with a skin burned terra-cotta red. He had fresh blue eyes and a candid set of features, and it was the combination of awkwardness and seeming simpleness that appeared to trouble the civilian guide. But all the sergeant said was, "I'll be along."

The general studied both men for a moment. Hounds carried a carbine, a revolver and a full belt of ammunition; he had a canteen and an improvised food pouch slung over a shoulder. The guide carried a carbine and apparently nothing more, but since he was well seasoned, the general did not presume to question him. He said, "It is a risky proposition and I wish you both luck," and shook hands with both of them. The sergeant saluted, Gervaise nodded and the two turned and passed along the streets of the various commands, the guide slightly in the lead.

A sergeant of the guard joined them and escorted them through the picket line and at last they left the security of the command behind, facing the troubled wilderness before them. A moon in the low southwest shed a strange-colored stain through the haze of fire smoke which covered the land, and Gervaise stood momentarily still, swinging his huge nose like a weathervane. "Likely to be some Sioux prowlers close by," he murmured. "They're fond of sneakin' close to a camp. We go soft for the next hour or so. Better throw away that canteen. Makes too much noise."

He moved on with so quick and soft a motion that Hounds temporarily lost him and made a racket with his boots in hurrying forward; and he knew the guide, who had no high opinion anyway of cavalrymen as scouters, would rate him down for it. He dropped the canteen from his shoulder, set his pace directly behind Gervaise; and thus they traveled with only the scrape of their boots on the gritty ground breaking the silence. The course was southward beside the dull streak of the river.

Presently the flare of Terry's campfires vanished behind the broken formations of the land, and the canyon of the Rosebud got deeper, and around them lay buttes and misshapen domes in the shadows, and day's heat still smoldered out of the soil. Now and then Gervaise made a soft grunt and stopped to crouch against the earth and to listen carefully. Hounds reckoned it was about two hours from camp when the guide descended into the Rosebud's canyon and again halted. The river at this point made a rustling racket over its shallowed gravel bed, and after a long pause Gervaise entered the water.

It was hip-high to the center and shoulder-high afterward; in a moment Gervaise's shadow disappeared and then with equal suddenness Frank Hounds stepped into the main channel and went down like a rock, weighted by his gear. He came up spitting and he gripped the carbine, grim as death, and made some effort to swim; he sank and he rose and he sank and he got to thinking it would be better if he let the carbine go, and it seemed he argued this point a long while and he couldn't bring himself to do it and then, his wind pretty well out of him, his feet at last hit bottom. He came to the far bank and stood alone in dense darkness, now shivering from the chill.

An owl hooted near by but it wasn't until the call came a second time that he caught on, and followed the sound of it and ran into Gervaise. The guide murmured, "Now we can make better time," and went away at his swift motion. They climbed from the Rosebud's canyon, struck a rocky, pitted bluff and continued with it. The direction was still south and the river was still beside them.

There wasn't much to do except to follow Gervaise, who moved on at a pace that was not far short of a trot; and now that there was time to think, the sergeant got to considering the chore ahead. There really wasn't any telling where Crook was to be found, and this shanks'-mare business might take them clear across the width of Montana. Crook had started from Fort Laramie with his command, marching north; Terry had started from the Missouri River, marching west. It was to be a sort of nutcracker business, the two columns pushing the Sioux ahead of them and then joining on Powder River and squeezing the Sioux between.

So far it hadn't worked out, for the Sioux slipped like water through Terry's fingers. Reaching the Rosebud, the general had sent Custer forward on scout and Custer, who was a hell-for-leather officer, had struck the Sioux trail and had pitched right in with five of his troops. That was the end of them all. The sergeant had been in the rescue party and he had come upon the field of Little Bighorn two days later, upon the bloated horses and the three hundred and fifty-two cavalrymen lying dead singly and in small clusters and in ragged windrows as the fury of the fight had caught them. That was why Terry was late in joining with Crook; and now Terry wanted to know why Crook was late, and where he was anyhow — and five thousand Sioux and Cheyenne under Sitting Bull and Gall and Crazy Horse swarmed this country like bees. Maybe the same thing had happened to Crook as had happened to Custer.

Around midnight Ned Gervaise stopped for

a brief breathing spell and thereafter moved forward. By three o'clock the sky had begun to pale, whereupon Gervaise turned about and backtracked a half mile. They ate raw bacon and hardtack and drank out of the river and climbed to a rocky crevice on the ridge crest just as daylight came.

"I'll take first watch," said the guide.

The sergeant sat down. His feet had swollen and filled his boots like lead, so that he could not remove them; and they ached as a tooth would ache. The civilian guide murmured, "For a cavalryman you're not bad," whereupon Hounds fell asleep.

Gervaise wakened him in the middle of the morning and took his own brief cat nap, never quite sleeping. The sun blazed down and the rocks began to soak up the heat and reflect it until the crevice became a bake oven and a smoky fog covered the land and ashes occasionally dropped and the smell of burning grass and pine got strong. "Sioux have set fire to the country," murmured Gervaise, "so's to ruin the forage for the cavalry horses."

"Ruins it for Sioux horses too," said Hounds.

"An Injun and his horse," said Gervaise, "can live a long time hungry."

By the middle of the afternoon the sergeant regretfully remembered his canteen; and since there was no more sleep possible both men sat in the crevice and watched the land before them. Throughout the day the sergeant had noticed faint streaks of dust and motion through the screen of smoke, which would be parties of Sioux on scout. "All hell boilin' around us," commented Gervaise, and was thoughtful.

Short of sunset, the guide's keen ears picked up some faint sound and he wiggled a warning hand to Hounds; ducked low in the crevice, Hounds presently watched a file of Sioux warriors race around the bend of the river and tilt down the bluff to the water's edge. They crowded their ponies into the water and for a moment were motionless. Sunlight flashed on the rifles they carried and gleamed on the polished bronze of their bare bodies. They were a handsome lot, Hounds thought; they wore long black hair snagged with feathers and they had bold faces and looked upon the world as though they owned it.

The nearness of them turned his belly empty and hard and that was when he felt his fear. It wasn't so much the twenty-odd Sioux at the river that brought on the fear, for this crevice made a good bulwark and there was plenty of ammunition. The cold, hollow feeling came upon him from the sudden knowing that Gervaise and he were alone in the very heart of Indian country, surrounded by the wildest and keenest savage fighters on the continent.

The Sioux had come across the river and were directly below the crevice, talking among themselves; and one brave slid half down from his horse and stared at the earth. He was a tremendous Indian, better than six feet, Hounds judged, with a vast chest and thick arm and leg muscles. He straightened in the saddle, spoke a word, and led the band upriver around the bend.

"Close enough to smell 'em," murmured the sergeant.

"You'll smell 'em again," said Gervaise. "They struck our tracks. Those fellows are Cheyenne."

At sunset half an hour later Gervaise grunted another warning and in a little while the same band appeared on the farther bluff, filed into the canyon and crossed over, slowly riding down-river. The big Cheyenne kept his eyes fixed on the ground.

"They'll unravel the puzzle pretty soon," said Gervaise. "We got to get out of here."

Twilight was long and darkness was hard to wait for; and when at last Gervaise rose from the crevice he turned higher into the rough lands instead of descending to the river. Hounds made no mention of his thirst, which burned his throat and froze his tongue; reaching down he got a piece of rock and clapped it into his mouth and seemed to find relief.

They scrambled from rock to rock for the best part of two hours, until the sergeant's hands grew raw; and his feet seemed slick inside his boots, which puzzled him. The route took them higher so that they at last reached a point from which they looked out upon the black smoke-palled night and discovered distant campfires glowing. Gervaise paused to watch. "That's off by the Little Bighorn. Large camp. Well, we ain't makin' time. We'll cross the river and get out on flatter country."

They scrambled along the broken sides of the canyon to the river. Hounds flattened out and permitted himself only a short drink, and followed Gervaise steadily along the edge of the water through a narrow, black gorge whose walls picked up the river's murmuring and magnified it. Now and then as Gervaise paused and got to his knees to study the ground, the sergeant quenched his continued thirst carefully.

They crossed over at the first place the water made a racket on shallow gravel and this time Hounds loosened the gun sling and put it around his shoulders to have his arms free, but when he dropped over his depth and again fought his way half strangled ashore he decided it would be better to have the gun in a handier place to throw away if necessary. A man was always learning.

Gervaise had again halted and Gervaise put his mouth close to Hounds' ear, and whispered, "Wait here," and faded into the downstream blackness.

Hounds crouched against the bluff, quietly shaking from the water's chill. He got his bacon out of the pouch and ate it raw and was displeased with its rancid taste and returned to the river for a final drink. Somewhere in the direction Gervaise had gone, a single dull, grunting echo rose and played out into the rustling of the river; flat on the gravel, Hounds strained his ears into the silence and caught a brief gritting echo of feet. That would be Gervaise coming back. But the sound ceased and the minutes went by and at last Hounds lifted himself from the gravel and stepped carefully on.

The smell of fire smoke ran down this gorge strongly and the rustle of the river over its ford continued. Stepping forward at a faster pace — because now he felt the fear of loneliness — he saw the dull shadow of the river bulked against him and his foot struck something inside the sandy soil, and he jumped back a full pace and stood still. Sweat broke out like needles all over his body and he brought his carbine's muzzle around and crouched until the shock wore off. Dropping to his knees he crawled forward and touched the soft bulk his foot had struck, and ran his hands over a man's body.

The man wore clothes and the clothes were warm; and then he knew this was Gervaise. He dropped his head until he saw the pallid shine of the guide's face and the blood streaking in it, and the broken remnants of Gervaise's skull.

He reared back like a runner crouched and listened to the river's murmuring. This had happened within twenty feet of him less than five minutes before; and the savage was somewhere about. But he heard nothing and he saw nothing in the smoky black and the urge to get out of the canyon lifted him as though he had no weight and turned him against the bluff wall. He found footholds in the rock and rose up a matter of twenty feet or more to a first shelf and now, in full flight, he ran along this shelf until he reached a ridge to a broken area and crouched low in the rocks.

He rose to orient himself, but he could not long stand still because of the constant throb of his feet; and so he threaded the piled-up rocks of the ridge, moved down a slope to what seemed like a broad sage and bunch-grass plain and pointed south. It was now maybe ten o'clock, with thirty miles before him and no wiry little man to set a pace; therefore the sergeant stretched out his legs and set his own pace. He missed the wiry little man.

As he strode forward he saw the vague shape of a glow high to his right. The farther he traveled the greater that glow became until at last near midnight the upper sky was a vast bloodstain. He got to thinking about it, remembering that the highest land near by was the massive bulk of the Bighorn Range; and, when he recollected that, he felt surer of himself — for the Bighorns were in the west where they should be and his course was right.

He stepped in a coulee for a brief rest and continued. Sometime before daybreak he identified an Indian camp by the sound of dogs barking, and he cut a circle around the camp and came to a stream he believed to be the Tongue. He had little idea of its width or its depth and he followed its bank upstream with daylight not far away until he heard dogs barking again. He had skirted one camp and now confronted another; and probably was in the center of a whole area of sleeping Indians. Wading into the river as far as his waist, he saw the outline of the far shore and felt doubtful. Halfway across, the river bottom went out beneath him and he sank; and when he came up, the current pushed him downstream rapidly and he let the carbine go and began to swim with the weight of his clothes and his revolver and gunbelt pulling strongly at him. The current broke into short waves, whereupon he let his feet down and touched bottom and walked this way a short distance and again stepped over his head.

The current ran fast. When he struggled to the surface he was close by the south shore and he could distinguish a dull white circle of tents on the bank and, in the unsettled darkness which precedes morning, a squaw bent over a small fire; he took his deep breath and sank and let the current carry him, even though his feet grated on the river's bottom. The next time he rose he was below the camp and he got a footing and left the river.

He was a hundred feet below this camp and saw other squaws now coming from their tents. Eastward, a crack of light drove its wedge between earth and sky; and before him stood a string of buttes, toward which he immediately moved. By the time he reached the foot of the buttes a morning twilight had come upon the land and one quick glance behind him showed other villages scattered up and down the Tongue and other fires sheering their bright points upward. He fell into a crease of the buttes, fast climbing; he faded back into them and reached a summit from which in all directions the land spread out.

He was still adrip and now he had his forethought of the burning day to come and took off his shirt and wrung the water from it, tinged though it was from dust and sweat and from the blue dye of the shirt, into the crown of his campaign hat. Once the butte had been square-topped and now was broken away so that it was a series of small potholes exposed to the sky; in one of these potholes he rested and watched the camp below him come to life and grow active. What he had come upon was a sizable wing of the whole Sioux nation camped here in a series of small villages and while he watched he noticed scouts ride in fast and other groups whirl out. Breakfast fires spotted the valley for a mile up and down the river, and tents began to fall and horsemen trotted into the plain and by sunrise all these people were traveling east with their dust making its heavy clouds around them.

He laid his back against the rim of the pothole and he closed his eyes against the streaming impact of the sun, and then he felt heat soak into him and he opened his eyes and found the sun well up in the sky, and knew that he had slept. When he realized that, he felt fear again. His legs ached up into his knees and he had no particular feeling around his toes. Two nights afoot in the rocks had worn the boot soles thin and in places had broken them. The bottoms were stained red, so that he knew then what the feeling of wetness had been; but when he tried to remove the boots he could not.

Heat poured into the pothole, and the rocks burned when he touched them, and the air was so thin that he could not satisfy his lungs, and his heart labored for the want. Out to the north a cloud rose from the earth, small but growing; to westward the large Sioux party kicked up its departing dust. For a little while the valley of the Tongue was deserted, but around noon other parties of horsemen poured down from the Bighorns and whirled along the river, passing at the foot of his butte; and other Sioux groups scudded out of the south. The country around him boiled with its dust smoke as the generals of these people — Sitting Bull and Gall and Crazy Horse and the lesser chiefs — feinted and confused their tracks by constant motion, and boldly maneuvered. The death of Custer had made them ambitious.

By the middle of the afternoon he knew he had to do something about his feet; the ache thundered up from his heels to his hips and was worse than the pain of hot irons. He got out his knife and cut away the leather tops from knee to ankle, and he made a small opening along the back edge of the leather just above the heel to relieve the growing pressure. More than this he figured he couldn't do, for if he loosened them more he would lose them when he walked again. As he bent at this chore he caught the fetid odor from them; it was not a smell of sweat and it was not a healthy smell.

Later he tried the water in his hat, which by now had evaporated to a jellylike scum, and found he could not swallow it.

The dust to the north grew into a small group of Sioux leisurely advancing upon the river. Reaching it, they stopped for water and were close enough for him to spot one huge shape on a pony and to recognize the massive Cheyenne. This one did some talking, after which the party rode upriver a mile or more, crossed over and came back.

The sergeant was not then greatly troubled, for the movement of the Indian villages had erased his own bootprints which, he guessed, the small party had been following all the way from the Rosebud. They came downriver, reading the ground, and they circled the butte and searched the land on that side and came back again to the river where after a moment's pause the big Cheyenne stared above him at the row of buttes closely, cried a single shrill word and wheeled upriver again, disappearing in the broken country.

As they disappeared, another long file appeared from the west — men, women and children and ponies — and moved along the river until they were below the sergeant, and here stopped to set up camp. The sun went down, and in the twilight the sergeant saw the Indian fires dance and heard the thin clack of camp talk and watched a single buck lead four horses away from camp and leave them on picket.

Now he turned his eyes southward toward low hills he had long been watching, hoping to find the far-off glitter of Crook's fires. But he saw nothing and sighed a little as he thought of the night's march to the Powder, forty miles away. In the darkness he ventured to stand on his legs — and fell back at once and knew there would be no more walking for a while. His feet had played out.

The camp settled down and the fires faded. Near ten o'clock he left the pothole, crawled gingerly down the sliding rubble of the butte and stopped at the edge of the river meadow, the four horses grazing a hundred feet away.

The dogs had been making a racket in the night, and continued on. Well wrapped in the shadows, he observed that the camp seemed indifferent. Earlier a band of soldier warriors had circled the butte on a kind of guard mission but there were no other pickets around camp. He remembered, as he drew his knife and opened it, that Indians mounted from the off side of a pony, and he stood straight up and drew his lips hard against his teeth from the shock of his feet and stepped forward full stride at the horses. They stopped grazing when he was twenty feet away and they stepped sidewise until they faced him.

He seized one picket rope and slashed it and worked up the rope to the horse's head and made a guttural murmur, but even then he found it unnatural to mount from the off side and had to put himself to it; he seized the pony's mane with a good grip, drew his mouth together and made the necessary spring. As soon as he hit the back of the pony he was moving away, using his legs and the picket rope to maneuver with. He had a tremendous desire to set off at full gallop but he held the impulse down until he had made a complete circle of the butte; and then he hit the pony with the end of the picket rope and streaked south. Behind him he thought maybe there was some extra noise but he was not too sure.

The night and its smoke were as bad as before and he had to trust the pony for the lay of the land. Four or five miles south of the buttes he drew in and listened and heard nothing at all, and went on into country which required slower going. He crossed a creek and felt the bulk of the Bighorns nearer and caught the heat and the ashes of the fire up there. It was the smell of fire that veered the pony constantly so that the sergeant had to fight it back as he approached the low silhouette of rougher country. He struck the creek again and, since the creek seemed to head up in this rough country, he followed it and found a defile through the broken rocks and rising ridges and came to a kind of summit.

What he saw ahead of him made him stop, for though he was not a sentimental man the sight of fires burning half a mile before him — the neat rows of army fires — made him think of many strange things which had no particular bearing on the night; and he thought, too, that it was hard on Gervaise to be the one who didn't get through and that a man never rightly knew what his luck was like or the length of his days, and that maybe it was better that way anyhow. He even ceased to think of the bone-deep flares of pain in his legs as he put the horse down a dry watercourse with the army fires straight ahead.

It was in the exact jaws of these rocks, with the lights of Crook's camp making bright lanes across the flat surface of Powder River, that a gun flashed bright before him and a shot rolled out like an explosion from a hollow tub and the pony broke gait and the sergeant went over its head and struck the rocky earth and rolled on through a roar and a rush of thunder.

He was thirty feet from the rocks when he stopped and what kept him conscious was the smell of danger as strong as the smell of ammonia. The feet of the ambusher now crushed along the rocks at him and as the sergeant came to his knees he watched the shadow of that man grow heavier and taller before him, and lifted his gun on the shadow. But he thought it might be an out-stationed picket of Crook's command and so he shouted, "Hey, soldier," and when he got no reply he fired twice at the shadow and heard it grunt and drop. He was on his feet and he trotted back and stooped long enough to make out the giant shape of the Cheyenne who had followed him so far, and then another gun howled from the rocks and the sergeant swung and raced for the river.

A corner of his mind had room enough for self-reproach. As Gervaise had said, the dangerous spot was just at the edge of an army command where the Sioux liked to lie waiting; and he had forgotten that. He heard another shot behind.

Across the river was the sharp halloo of an officer's commands, and when he reached the river he ran straight into it and expected to sink out of sight. But this was the Powder, which was shallower than a farmyard duck pond, and he never got to the depth of his knees at any place.

A sentry on the opposite shore shouted, "Halt — who's there," and fired at him, and shouted again, "Sergeant of the guard, post five!" The sentry's bullet was a wind at the sergeant's ears as he cried back, "You can quit that, soldier."

"Never mind the guard!" bawled the sentry and trotted to the edge of the stream. The sergeant floundered from the water, dropped to his face and lay gasping on the ground.

He was inside Crook's lines, with a guard detail coming up. He crouched on his knees and hands with his head bent down and he turned around and ducked his head under the water and felt better. Somebody got hold of his arms and pulled him up, and meanwhile a file of cavalry rushed over the river at the rocks.

"Dispatch for Crook," breathed the sergeant. "This Crook's outfit?"

An officer strode from the night and said, "Come with me," and led him back through lines of supply wagons drawn up like a barricade at the river, past troop streets and horses on picket lines, and down a row of officers' tents to one tent which sat by itself and faced the whole command. The general, aroused by the racket, stood under the tent's fly — a man of medium height, with a sharp-seamed face and a long fanned-out beard. The sergeant had seen pictures of him and knew him at once; and came to a stand and made a regular parade-ground salute.

"Sergeant Hounds, F Troop, Second Cavalry." He hauled Terry's letter from his hind pocket and presented it. "Dispatch from General Terry."

Crook held the dispatch in his hand, meanwhile considering the sergeant. Light came out of the general's tent and illuminated the sergeant's sun-swollen face, his scorched eyes, his cracked lips. The sergeant's shirt and trousers were gray with alkali and sweat and when the sergeant stepped back a pace he left his footmarks as a pair of red stains on the ground.

"You came through alone?" said Crook.

"There was a guide," answered the sergeant. "He didn't make it."

The general seemed inclined to question the sergeant further, but he knew when a man was dead beat, and so turned to one of his officers: "Bourke, attach this man to G Troop. See that he gets something to eat and new boots. Thank you, sergeant."

The sergeant made a pivot and felt the raw quiver of his feet. The officer was beside him

131

as they walked down through the camp; and the river was close by. The sergeant said, "With your permission, sir," and went to the river and sat down. He got out his knife and he cut the rest of the boots from his feet; other men and officers had moved up and these stood by him, and Bourke bent over and stared at the sergeant's feet and swore to himself. "I'm going to have a couple men carry you to the doctor, sergeant. It looks as if it was a hard trip."

The sergeant plunged his feet into the Powder and was eternally grateful for the water's coolness. He stared over the river, and now he remembered Gervaise again and he put his mind to the guide, recollecting the tone of the guide's voice and the shape of his small body in the black shadows of the land. It seemed a long time back. By the clock it was just about twelve hours ago, but by the things which had happened it was as good as a year. Maybe, thought the sergeant, there was more than one kind of time; some day he'd have to stop and think about that. But meanwhile the men around him seemed to expect him to say something of what had happened and he searched his mind with a good deal of care and found very little that could be properly said aloud. For the things of most importance, now that he thought of it, were things he had felt inside of him, like waves of warmth and sharp shocks of ice, and the images that were so clear before him were all very strange and would sound foolish when they were put to words. In a thing like this a man was pretty much alone.

But the men still waited and so, after a long pause, he said, "On a scout a man ought to wear shoes that fit him and he ought to carry tobacco to cut his thirst." Then, as a final concession to their curiosity, he waved his hand northward: "Lot of Indians over there."

On Texas Street

Eighteen hundred Star Cross cattle, lean and wild from the long drive out of Texas, went bawling down the stockyards' runway in Abilene. This was the end of the trail for the ten men standing by the gate, but they waited the word of Major MacBeath, who watched them with a critical amusement.

"We start back home in a couple days," he said. "Meanwhile let me remind you this is the wickedest town in the West and Tom Smith the toughest marshal along the trail. I wouldn't advise tearin' Abilene apart. It's been tried."

Lee Bowie nodded and turned immediately away. The rest of the crew broke after him but he went on alone at a rapid gait, as though hurrying toward a definite objective, the late sun throwing his high, straight shadow out into the deep dust. A few houses and a railroad track lay over in this quarter of town and the day's heat pressed down on a seeming emptiness. Yet it was a spurious emptiness, for two blocks onward he turned a corner and was stopped by the impact of a turbulent current of life rolling between a double row of flare-fronted stores, boiling along sidewalks that rose and fell in front of each building.

He had never been in Abilene before, but the legends of this town stretched far down the trail and so what he saw here was familiar. This was the blood-red heart of wicked Abilene, this single block of Texas Street. On his left stood the Alamo saloon, which was Wild Bill Hickok's headquarters; at the farther bend of the street stood the Bullshead and the Old Fruit — and beyond were the more shadowy tenements where the trail hand took his chances, without recourse. This was the man-eating cattle depot whose roar sounded all down the dusty leagues of unfenced and lonely plain.

He had come to a stand, Lee Bowie, his gravely blue eyes showing a faint glitter of excitement. A heavy traffic in and out of the Alamo's doors swayed him a little and moved him to the edge of the walk. Men of his own fraternity, dark and rash and full-blooded, strolled restlessly by. The Star Cross crowd turned the corner and Swamp Humbird's voice ripped through this confusion. "Here's the first stop." Star Cross filed solidly into the Alamo and the open doors let out a gush of sound, but Lee Bowie went on up and down the uneven sidewalk until he reached a grocery store. He turned in here, his big spurs scraping up minute jets of metal sound. Afternoon shadows dimmed the place, the smell of food was very keen. A storekeeper stood at a counter, watching him.

"I want a dozen apples," said Lee Bowie. The storekeeper said, "Apples," and moved away. Lee Bowie stood straight on the balls of his feet; he made a sharp figure in this room and his extreme quietness was like a signal echoing across the lesser quiet. He was a man ridden down to leanness and to violent hungers and the flatness of his body was the flatness of suppressed energy. The storekeeper returned, laying a paper sack on the counter. He stared at Lee Bowie. He meant to speak, but a woman's voice, very soft, crossed Lee Bowie's shoulders. It said:

"Will you get me a pound of flour, Mr. Herrick?"

A boy in an apron appeared from somewhere. The storekeeper said, "A pound of flour for Ilena Tillman, Johnny." He turned his eyes back to Lee Bowie and spoke in a manner carefully avoiding offense.

"It is a rule in Abilene to deposit your guns while here. I'll be glad to handle them for you."

Lee Bowie removed his hat. Then he turned. He hadn't any notion of speaking to a woman he didn't know; it was only a courtesy as grained in him as the pigment of his skin. Her voice struck soft and pleasant tones that made pure melody to a man whose life ran so remotely from women. He looked at her with a directness he could not help; he stood very still and a little stiff, holding himself out of her way. A perceptibly reddish hair fell down across his forehead and the faint wildness of his young southern blood brightened his blue glance. He saw her clearly and in detail, as he saw everything.

She was a slim girl, with eyes that were neither afraid of him nor interested in him. Her lips were firm across an oval, sober face, and her breathing slowly stirred the round, definite curve of her breasts. But she watched him as she might have watched a wall and he understood instantly, because she was a northern townswoman and he a puncher off the trail, how far apart they were. He pulled his glance away, knowing he could not in politeness look longer.

"The guns," suggested the shopkeeper.

"Whose rule is that?"

"Marshal Smith's."

"I do not doubt you," said Lee Bowie courteously, "but I believe I shall wait for him to tell me."

He went out, walking with the perceptible

roll of a dismounted horseman, into the steady boil of life on Texas Street. He stood against a hitching rack and took an apple from the sack and all the dry and starved appetite of the dusty trail rushed out of him to savor the fruit's delicacy; when he bit it the pleasure was so keen that a stinging sensation cramped his jaw muscles. This was why his long legs had carried him down Texas Street in such a hurry.

The Star Cross crew came swinging out of the Alamo and broke into fragments that drifted with the street's flowing stream. Swamp Humbird drove his barrel-chested body straight along the uneven walk, making way for nobody. Drink had loosened him up and his heavy white teeth flashed against the almost negroid darkness of his skin. Behind him, a faithful and loyal shadow, walked the Star Cross Kid, Bill Teeters. They came up to Lee Bowie and halted. Swamp Humbird said, with a vast amusement: "Who said it was a tough town? Come on. We got a lot of joints to look at yet."

Lee Bowie's glance divided itself thoughtfully between the two. Swamp Humbird was a tough one who would presently be looking for trouble. A wild brute only one grade above the wild brutes he herded, he made bad company for Bill Teeters, who was soft clay yet to be formed.

"It's supper time," said Lee Bowie, and looked at Bill Teeters. "Better come with me and chuck a feed under your belt."

Swamp Humbird's big teeth flashed a grin. "Time enough for that. It's this Bullshead joint we want to see."

Lee Bowie carefully placed his sack of apples on the walk, excitement creeping along his nerves. A gray horse appeared at the bend of Texas Street and came onward carrying a square, chunky man who wore a star on his vest. Marshal Tom Smith, of course. Lee Bowie's eyes brightened perceptibly; his lips came together. Tom Smith turned and reined his horse. He was fair-skinned and wonderfully built and a dark mustache bordered a strong, steady mouth and he sat in his saddle with an ease that was impressive. He had a presence that suddenly reached out and warned both Swamp Humbird and the kid. They turned instantly around. It was that definite.

Tom Smith said: "Oblige me, gentlemen, by putting up your guns with the most convenient storekeeper. It is a rule of the town."

It was soft and agreeable; it was as bland as a breath of summer's breeze. But Lee Bowie straightened away from the porch pillar and a livelier interest strengthened his glance. He watched Tom Smith's gray eyes very carefully. Swamp Humbird suddenly laughed and walked around the hitch rack into the dust. His lip corners dropped as he stared up at Smith.

"You're the terror of the town? Mister, nobody gets my guns."

This was Humbird's mistake, Lee Bowie thought — to confuse that drawling humility of speech with fear. Tom Smith reined his horse over against Humbird with a single motion. His gloved hand swept down and cracked into Humbird's temple; he was off his horse so rapidly that Lee Bowie's vision barely caught the sequence of action. His fist smashed Humbird again and Humbird was down in the dust, with Tom Smith bending over him, getting his gun.

Bill Teeters moved and his arm started to drop toward his belt, whereupon Lee Bowie threw his hand across the kid and stopped that gesture. He said coldly: "Don't be a sucker." But he never took his glance off the marshal and when Tom Smith wheeled about Lee Bowie saw what he wanted to see. The pleasantness was gone; what burned dangerously in Tom Smith's eyes now was the devil's own temper — a temper that slept until called upon and then became utterly unmerciful. Lee Bowie's hand still lay across Bill Teeter's nervous arm and this Tom Smith noticed with a cold, gripping attention. His eyes examined Lee Bowie; their glances definitely locked and they stood still, thus visually exploring each other, a small crowd standing around them. Swamp Humbird got to his feet, no word coming from him. His face was brutally drawn, his lips were stretched.

Lee Bowie reached over and unbuckled the kid's belt; and he unbuckled his own. "That's all right," he told Tom Smith softly. "We'll store the guns."

Tom Smith nodded and turned to his horse, carrying Humbird's gun. He swung to the saddle and went on down the exact center of the street, his broad back turned on them. Humbird flashed a hating glance at that back. He said, "We'll see! Come on, kid."

"Never monkey with a soft-speakin' man," murmured Lee Bowie and wheeled toward the store. The crowd gave ground to let him through; and then he saw Ilena Tillman standing with her shoulders against the store wall, the aroused and speculative interest of her glance crossing the distance to strike him powerfully. He went on into the store, left the guns and came out. She had gone.

The sun was down and a faint violet had begun to flow through the air as Lee Bowie went to an adjacent restaurant for supper.

When he came out, a cigar clenched between his teeth, deep dusk had settled across Abilene. He had eaten well and the savor of the smoke pleasantly soothed him; and he stood at the corner of the Alamo in the manner of a spectator, watching night come to Texas Street. Lights brightened the walks. Music of a sort began to rise from the far bend where stood the Old Fruit and the Bullshead.

Gently amused, he watched the tide thicken, he heard the growling undertone deepen. His own kind were crowding into this short lane. Lean and reckless men thirsty for trouble; and the other kind waited for them — the gambler, the barkeeper, the harpy, the slugger. The townspeople had withdrawn to the quiet backwaters of Abilene, the respectable trade was done. In the space of an hour Texas Street had turned into a jungle where men prowled at their own risk, where Tom Smith aloofly rode on a gray horse and was concerned with only the slimmest threads of order.

Lee Bowie wheeled back around the corner and paced indolently toward the stockyards, the shadows at once covering him, the embroiled sounds subsiding as he left the Alamo corner behind. The stillness and the scent of the prairie reached in; ahead of him winked the lights of the fashionable Drovers' Rest. On his right hand, obscure and peaceful, lay the residential district. Deep in ease, he turned idly that way, his cigar making a fragrant wake behind. Flat echoes rose from his treading and troubled the silence of this region and then died out; and yellow windows glowed behind picket fences and he saw families sitting around quiet supper tables. Somewhere an organ softly sighed a tune. The growl of Texas Street, where he properly belonged, was only a murmur in this world which he now passed through as a spectator.

It puzzled him to find that he had stopped and placed his hands on a pointed gate post — that he looked now through one of those cheerful windows and felt a strange stirring in him he could not explain. There was a thought running oddly through his head. "I am twenty-five. I have never been inside a home like that since my mother died." A faint thread of wind came up from the south, carrying a call that he heard and understood. But a feeling flowed powerfully through the gentle dark and touched him and struck one deep chord of loneliness. The ease of the night was gone and a hunger was in him again, strange and compelling.

Somewhere behind him lifted the quick thin wail of a child, crying, so imperative that he swung abruptly around and saw the opening brightness of a doorway across the street. A man stumbled out of that doorway, short and broad and bearded, and he was saying impatiently, "No — no — no!" A woman followed, hands folding and unfolding themselves in her apron. She called after him. "Henry!" But the man turned on the walk and strode unevenly down the darkness toward Texas Street a block onward. Lee Bowie saw his odd shape reach that bright area and push through the crowd toward the Bullshead. The child had ceased to cry, but the woman still stood on the porch and her low, weary sighing crossed the street to oppress Lee Bowie bitterly.

His cigar no longer pleased him. He threw it into the dust and paced soberly on. He murmured, "You're a fool." In Abilene was a dividing line as definite as a stripe painted across the earth and when he left the shadows behind him and entered the alive current of Texas Street he felt he had passed beyond it. There was an appetite in him he could not identify — there was a concern in him he could not identify. It propelled him across the street into the boiling confusion of the Bullshead. A great mirror flashed out light and all the walls threw back the collected rumble of the crowd. Bill Teeters and Swamp Humbird stood at the bar. Going toward them, between the well-filled gaming tables, he saw in Swamp Humbird's eyes a smoldering remembrance of the beating Tom Smith's fists had administered. Humbird's heavy lips stirred. "We'll see — we'll see!"

But Lee Bowie wasn't listening. The short, bearded man sat at a table in the middle of the room, already drunk, counting a stack of chips passed him by a slim, scrupulously sad player opposite. Lee Bowie studied all the men around that table and knew them well for what they were, and his eyes went back to the slim one — a gambler in every secretive gesture. An impulse, rash and heady, moved him toward that table. He put a hand on the bearded fellow's shoulder. "Colonel," he said, "there's a man outside that wants to see you."

The bearded one looked up, displeased. "My name is Wesser," he said, "and I don't know you."

Lee Bowie scarcely heard. His glance was pinned to the slim gambler, who stared back and showed the faint lip curl of a dog deprived of its bone. Bowie said to the gambler, "Get yourself another sucker, brother," and lifted Wesser with a sudden force and pushed him toward the door. One sharp word ripped at him from behind and when he looked about he saw the gambler rising and pointing. Sudden wildness rushed through Lee Bowie and he heard his own rash laughter run across the room's dying confusion. Swamp Humbird moved slowly through the crowd toward the gambler's table, eager for a fight; and Bill Teeters came obediently behind him. Lee Bowie shoved Wesser out of the Bullshead and across the street without consideration. A quick crash pursued them and at once the Bullshead began to emit a rising hum of anger. Lee Bowie, in the shadows beyond Texas Street, stopped his man. He reached out and slapped Wesser smartly across the face. He said, dismally outraged: "You're drunk and you're a damned fool."

"I don't know you," complained Wesser. "I have just lost fifty dollars back there."

"Leave those joints alone, Colonel," said Lee Bowie. "Leave 'em for suckers like me. Your fifty dollars is gone."

Wesser shook his shoulders, but Lee Bowie pushed him on without effort. They went down the vague line of picket fences, into the Wesser yard. They walked up to the porch.

"I'll leave you, Colonel —"

He got no farther. For the door opened and a woman stood there — Wesser's wife, Bowie supposed. Her head lifted and her lips moved and Lee Bowie, removing his hat, felt ashamed at seeing the naked expression of relief in her eyes. He said: "The Colonel and I got to talk-

147

ing about old times. I am sorry to disturb you."

Wesser rolled into the room. He sat down in the nearest chair, doggedly repeating: "I have lost fifty dollars."

The woman said, swiftly releasing her breath: "Is that all, Henry?"

Lee Bowie heard none of this. His glance had lifted across the room and he found Ilena Tillman standing quietly there, watching him with a directness that was like a command. Lee Bowie murmured, "I will not trouble you," and moved slowly backward. He heard Ilena Tillman speaking to the woman. She said, "It is all right now," and came quickly out of the house, closing the door. Her slender silhouette strengthened beside him and the fragrance of her presence locked his speech. When he went down the steps she was beside him. There was a soft, slow melody in the way she talked.

"He had a thousand dollars in his pocket and he might have lost it all. He's been drunk since morning. When he wakes up tomorrow he'll be full of shame."

"Men," he said quietly, "should stay where they belong. Wesser has no business in the Bullshead. That's a place for fellows like me."

There was a bubbling of sound on Texas Street; but the shadows here were still, with

148

that strange feeling coming out of the dark again to disturb him. Ilena Tillman's voice was slow and full and considering. "I live across the street," she said and turned, darkness swirling around her. Lee Bowie stood in his tracks. But she looked back at him and the round white oval of her face lifted. He walked on with her then and stopped at the vague opening of a gate, recklessness rising; something was happening here — something he didn't know.

"Today you rode up from the south. Tomorrow you'll ride back into it."

"Yes," he said.

Her murmur was soft; it was mysterious. "Always the trail — always Texas Street and a saloon?"

"I'll never make Wesser's mistake and stray outside my proper limits."

"There are other ways of living."

"They are not for me."

She said: "You have been kind to the Wessers. Come to supper at our house tomorrow night. We eat at seven."

"It would be a mistake."

The thready breeze came off the wild plain like a summons; on Texas Street was a gunshot, with a quick clashing of voices. But he stood here and felt the strong undertow unsettling him. The melody of this girl's voice and her presence stirred him indescribably, rousing the suppressed hungers he had thought to quench on Texas Street.

"Are you afraid?"

"I'll come," he said.

She turned through the gate and was gone. But her words lifted on a tone of gayety: "Good night."

He wheeled and returned to the brightness of Texas Street, walking into its full flood. Many men were slowly backing away from the Bullshead and Tom Smith paced across the dust on his gray horse. He saw Lee Bowie and reined around and stopped at the edge of the sidewalk, looking down with an unruffled and inflexible courtesy.

"Your two friends got a little excited in that rumpus you started. I am forced to give you the warning I gave them. Be out of Abilene by sundown tomorrow night."

Lee Bowie laughed abruptly. He said, "I may be," and felt Tom Smith's glance tear through him. The man nodded and went riding down the exact middle of the street.

He sat on the top rail of a stockyards corral, the long low flash of the afternoon's sun striking against him and engraving more sharply the soberness of his face. In another hour sunset would come, which was the time limit set by Tom Smith; and in another hour it would be seven o'clock, with Ilena Tillman waiting at her doorway. He had a decision to make here, with a trail leading into the far future from either of the two choices he might elect. He sat there inscrutably, his cool mind searching down those trails. In the south the yellow distances were turning faintly blue. Far off the dust of another advancing herd lifted high fumaroles of dust. Beyond lay the trackless plains. Over that wildness the wind would presently drift, bringing up messages to his attentive ears.

Major MacBeath marched down the dust from the Drover's Cottage. He stopped at the foot of the corral and studied Lee Bowie with a sharp understanding.

"You been perched there like a buzzard all afternoon. When I was a young man with time on my hands I never spent it in solitude. What's saloons and women for, Lee? You'll be old soon enough. Go get your fun while there's spice in it. Our business is done here. We head south after supper."

"I was born to the saddle and plenty of room to roam. It's a mistake to change. What would I be doin' as a townsman, Major?"

"Some doubt in your mind, Lee?"

"There was," mused Lee Bowie.

"You've got a cool head, Lee. You'll get along anywhere. Still, I'd hate to lose you."

"A man should stick to the tunes he can whistle," reflected Lee Bowie. "I'll be with you when it's time to go." He got down from the fence. He had made his decision and unaccountably it released his mind from strain and he strolled toward the bend of Texas Street with a feeling of ease, with the pungent scents of the day and the sharp angles of light and shadow registering keenly on his senses. In a little while he'd eat a dozen oysters at the restaurant, get his horse from the stable and drift into the southern shadows — back to the broad earth that held no puzzles for a man. At the corner of the Alamo he faced Henry Lewes, the Star Cross foreman.

Said Lewes: "I don't like what I see. Humbird's been actin' mysterious, over against the Bullshead, with Teeters apin' him like a shadow. I don't want to lug two empty saddles back over the Arkansas. Say somethin' to the kid."

"A cub wolf waitin' his turn to howl at the moon," murmured Lee Bowie and went on. Beyond the Alamo he stopped again to catch the details of a stage softly being set for trouble. Tom Smith rounded the bend on his big gray and traveled slowly down the middle of the dust, seeing nothing, seeing everything. He swung and vanished beyond the Bullshead. Over there, near the Bullshead doors, both

152

Swamp and Bill Teeters stood indifferently by, showing no apparent interest in the marshal as he passed. But this was only half the story to Lee Bowie, who turned his glance immediately across the way to the restaurant. There were three men watching him. Silent laughter stirred through him and the breath of coming events fed the wild and hungry blood in him. These were the gambler's dogs, out to tree him for dragging Wesser away from the poker table.

"Wesser was a fool," he thought, "for steppin' over to this side of Abilene. Wouldn't I be a fool to step over to his side? Men should stick to what they know."

The sun fell swiftly; and then it was dusk, blue shadows trickling across the housetops and lights flowing along the silver-yellow dust, with Texas Street slowly filling with restless men whose voices rose and grew different, whose muscles seemed to arch as they prowled. Respectability drew quietly back behind the picket fences of the side streets; and this narrow strip began to lift its jungle growl.

He felt himself change as well. Alert and attentive, his faculties sharpened to the secret maneuverings around him. The three men by the restaurant had faded — they had drawn mysteriously away from him; and down by the Bullshead, Swamp and the kid were now pacing into the darkness. The kid dropped into an alley's mouth, Swamp went on. Afterward Lee Bowie thought he knew how it would be and silently swore at the follies of ignorant men. He went forward at once, impelled by a sense of needed haste, cut across Texas Street and followed the Bullshead side wall to within a few yards of the alley. He stood in the deepening shadows staring into the heavier darkness of the street's end on his right, vaguely discerning Swamp Humbird's outline there.

What happened next was exactly as he guessed. Swamp's gun made a brash, red streak through the night and the report rushed wickedly across Abilene. Swamp yelled and fired again and afterward Lee Bowie heard the swift run of a horse coming along the other face of the Bullshead. Swamp was the bait to lure Tom Smith down this street, but it was the kid's hidden gun in the alley that would drop Smith as he passed by.

"A cub wolf waitin' to howl," he thought again, and saw Tom Smith round the corner of the Bullshead and trot forward. At that Lee Bowie slid the remaining yard along the boarded side of the Bullshead and flung himself into the alley. He plunged against the kid, who crouched there; his arm knocked aside the kid's lifted gun. He slapped the kid across the face, full of disgust, and heard Smith go

by the alley at a quick gallop. Swamp Humbird's gun roared again; and on the heels of
its dying echo there were two hard, booming
explosions nearer at hand, which was Tom
Smith's way of answering.

"I got to get to Swamp," said the kid,
breathing fast.

"Swamp's dead, kid. When did it get fashionable to shoot a man from shelter? You little
pup, you been drinkin' milk from the wrong
teat. Turn around and get down this alley or
you're dead too."

He turned Bill Teeters about and pushed
him forward; and then saw that way darker
than it should have been. For there were three
shadows filling the alley — and a man was
saying in a cold, bitter way, "You won't interfere with no more poker games —"

"Let 'em have it, kid," sighed Lee Bowie
and threw himself forward. He hit one of those
men full on, his flat chest striking and divert-
ing a sudden-rising arm, and he carried the
man on over into the rank back-door sweep-
ings of the Bullshead. Teeth bit wickedly into
his ear and a gun exploded along his leg. There
was no mercy in him then and no pity; he
cracked the man's belly with his knee and got
the gun from the man's hand and brought it
down over the vaguely rolling head he saw.
Hell seemed on the loose in this black slit;

155

powder smoke rolled its stifling way around him and sound slammed against the adjoining walls. The kid was crying, "Where you at, Lee?" And another fellow was bending over him to find a fair shot.

Lee Bowie rolled and slashed the barrel of the gun at the dim shine of the face he saw, and heard teeth and bones snap. The man fell on him heavily, without protest. The kid was creeping uncertainly forward. "Lee, where you at?" Behind, at the alley's mouth, Tom Smith's peremptory tones lifted: "Come out of there!" Lee Bowie crawled to his feet. He said, "Come on, kid," and ran into the depths of the alley; there was a right angle turn, and beyond it a sudden widening into a deserted corral where a line of wagons lay half dismembered. Lee Bowie stopped here.

The kid stood near him, his lungs reaching for air. "There was another one," he said unevenly. "I knocked him down."

Lee Bowie's laughter rubbed the darkness softly; it made the kid suddenly say, "What's funny?"

"Nothing, Bill. Anyhow, it isn't funny. You're through in Abilene. Go out of this corral and keep in the dark spots, all the way back to the stockyards. MacBeath will be waitin' there. Humbird's dead. Listen, pup — never fool with a quiet-speaking man."

"What's funny?" repeated Bill Teeters.

"I just thought of something. Get out of here before Smith comes."

He stood there, leaning his long frame against a wagon box, watching the kid walk awkwardly from the corral into the open prairie beyond. There was a camp fire burning yonder a quarter mile, cutting a pure orange hole against the black. Figures crouched around it; a steer bawled in the long distance. A breath of wind, aromatic with the wild lands it crossed, came into the corral. It would be like that down the trail — a red heart of fire burning beneath the black arch of the sky and a wind crossing the earth, and the chant of a coyote, wild and sad, in the mystery beyond.

He shook his head, thinking of things nearer to hand. Swamp was dead in the street and three men were crawling around a dark alley; and he stood here in this smelly obscurity and listened for pursuit. "The trail's long and it's wide. But it always comes to an end like this." He pushed himself away from the wagon and crossed the corral; he walked around the sagging skeleton of an old stable into Texas Street and followed it as far as the corner of the Bullshead. Lights blazed brighter here and the crowd stirred restlessly by him. A few men came back from that spot where Swamp had fallen; Abilene had forgotten about Swamp al-

157

ready. Tom Smith rode casually around the bend and saw Lee Bowie standing on the edge of the walk. He came over.

"Your twenty-four hours is up, friend," he said.

"It is why I am standing here," replied Lee Bowie, evenly and stubbornly polite. "My party has left Abilene by now. It is my intention to stay."

Tom Smith stared down and Lee Bowie saw the devil's temper in the man ruffle across his eyes. Never monkey with a quiet-speaking man. But it was a rule that worked both ways, as Lee Bowie hoped this marshal of Abilene would understand. He stood there, feeling Tom Smith's glance tear through him, matching that inflexible glance with a smooth, unbreakable calm.

Tom Smith inclined his head. He said then, in a manner of a man speaking to a known equal, "It is agreeable to me, friend," and turned his gray horse into the confused and yellow-patterned dust.

Lee Bowie wheeled, walking into the shadows at a rapid pace. He came to a picket fence and a quiet house lying behind it and for a moment he paused to look back again at Texas Street, a little wonder in his mind. Afterward he passed through the gate, going toward an open doorway that threw its full beam against

158

him. Ilena Tillman stood there and the sight of her slim shape against the light, so proud and so crowded with mystery for him, sent a sharp flash of excitement through Lee Bowie. He saw her lips move, he saw shadows suddenly die out of her eyes, and all at once there was a keenness in the night that stirred his hunger and made him reckless and richened all that he felt.

She said: "You were supposed to leave town tonight. But the trail couldn't pull you away."

He said, strangely moved: "I don't know why."

But she shook her head. There was a softness in her lips, an unfathomed light and warmth glowing out of her.

"It is something you will discover. Come in."

In Bullhide Canyon

It was another of those chases that wore badly on man and beast alike. At dusk of this desert eve — deep cobalt shadows running like water across the earth — Matt McQuestion halted his posse out in the wastelands and trained a severely blue glance against the masses of Bullhide Range twenty miles to the north. All those turret peaks and high black surfaces were fading behind the mysterious quality of night; full dark closed in even as he watched for some sign of Luke Daunnt and Luke's three henchmen — a dense dark, little relieved by the crystal brilliance of the stars above. Seeing it so, McQuestion turned in his seat and spoke to the ten vague forms behind:

"Swing straight east here and keep going. Camp twelve or fifteen miles away. When the sun comes up run north again, skirtin' the base of the range." And after a while his gently decisive voice added, "The idea is to raise dust yonder that Luke and his friends will see from the high ground on Bullhide. They'll judge we've missed the trail altogether."

161

One drowsy voice said: "Where'll you be, Sher'ff?"

"I'll continue this trail."

"When'll we be meetin' you?"

"Leave that to me," replied McQuestion and waited for the boys to go. There was more talk and a little show of resistance which he quelled with a slow "Hit the grit, now." Muffled protests drifted across the black as they filed away. McQuestion set his horse to a sedate canter along the original trail, chuckling softly to himself and feeling at once a greater freedom of movement. He had been trying to get rid of the posse for two days. It had worried and fretted him, as all posses worried this gray old lone wolf who had led perhaps a hundred of them on the heels of one renegade or another. Inevitably they were composed of energetic young men out to make a holiday affair of something they knew nothing about.

"Sprawlin' all over the landscape like puppy dogs," he reflected. "Now that the distance is narrowin' down, one of those lads would rove too far aside and get killed, which only makes the record of disaster so much the worse. I've seen it happen before. Manhuntin' is for an old sinner like me who knows what the other sinner is goin' to do and can beat him to the doin' of it."

The frame of mind presently astonished

him, and it came to him that he was getting old. In other days sudden death had seemed of less consequence. Now it filled him with a deep regret; and those boys he had sent away were too young to die at the hands of Luke Daunnt. It took age to discern that youth was a precious, irreplaceable thing. Meanwhile, a deep arroyo advanced out of the night and he dismounted in it to build up a little fire of sage stems, over which he boiled his coffee in a tomato can. Coffee and a dry bacon sandwich made his supper. Afterwards he pulled a ragged slip of paper from a pocket and smoothed its surface against his boot. He had read this note from Sheriff Till Tayloe of the adjoining county before but he read it again with that patient inquisitiveness which seeks a deeper and deeper meaning:

MATT: No sleep for sixteen hours and this written while somebody holds a match over me. Party of five came into Rainwater last evening and hit the bank as Colonel Gooch and his cashier was about to close. Cashier folded like a lily but Gooch was a woolly bear and they killed him cold when he reached. We dropped a kid with a thumb missing. Others got off though we saw one shiver from a direct hit. Lost the trail two, three times. On it now but don't know which way it's going. Chances are they'll come your way. If so, I'll be with you in ten hours. Meanwhile, get your lads in action. These fellows all unknown to me. In haste.

"TILL TAYLOE."

"But not unknown to me," mused McQuestion, replacing the note. "The kid with the missing finger was Bud Malloy and that spots the others. Bud got under Luke Daunnt's bad influence two years ago. So it is Luke in front of me, and Luke's party is Earl Shaneways, Slash Bill Evans and Yuma the half Navajo. Not an ounce of mercy in any. It's a wonder they didn't kill the cashier on principle."

Cross-legged before the waning fire, Matt McQuestion's slim military body revealed no fatigue. Nor did his face, which had little on it to reveal the thirty years of his hunting profession; it was a smooth, rather studious face and would have seemed clerkly save for the long sweep of jawbones. Underneath silvered brows that were like veritable awnings was a pair of faded blue eyes now abruptly hardened from thought; below a neat and grizzled mustache his lips made a firm, long line.

"No mercy in any of 'em," he repeated slowly. "And I can't have another killin'. This job's got to be finished completely."

Rising then, he stamped out the remnant of fire and got to his horse. Beyond the arroyo he settled to another deliberate pace, heading straight north once more without haste. There was never any need of haste. Over a hundred trails and across the years he had learned that. Long, long ago a wise man had written the fate of the transgressor in the Book of books — and Matt McQuestion had seen the inexorable sentence work out too often to doubt it. So, cantering under the starlight, soothed by this loneliness that he understood and loved so well, he came against the suggested weight of the Bullhide parapets about midnight. One slight roll of earth lifted him toward the more distinct presence of the rugged hills. The scent of a risen dust was in the air.

"They've been tarryin' for somethin'," he observed to himself.

But a little later he lost the smell of that dust and back-tracked to meet it again. The fresher trail took him along a corridor with heightening sides; then the dust smell died utterly and a slow stream of wind washed across his face. Suddenly he was confronted by a vast doorway in those sheer walls striking up to the sky. Bullhide had its canyon, of which this grim aperture was the mouth.

"They've gone in here," he muttered, a

little surprised, "instead of takin' the high ground. Odd. I wouldn't of done it. Eight miles to the first side trail out of this trap. Thirty miles to the end."

Halted, he was thinking now as those four outlaws would be thinking. He placed himself in their shoes, assumed their fears and their animal instincts. And an unaccustomed hardness of temper came to this wise old steward as he thought of those wild ones disturbing the peace of his county, rousing the blood lusts of the youngsters.

"It's got to end," he murmured. "Luke and me have out-lived our time. West ain't as wild as it used to be and the rule of quickest gun is going out, thank God. But Luke doesn't know it. He's a relic of a wilder West and he walks among ghosts, same as me. But it won't do — it won't do. I don't propose to let the wolf call ring across Bullhide again. Well, I'm an old hound dog that's been snoozin' in front of a comfortable fire. Wonder if I've still got a nose for scent."

The delay was only of a few moments' duration, yet in that length of time he had reverted to a state of mind at once keen, cold and unsentimental. He was now a hunter, nothing else. Turning, he retreated from the canyon's mouth, attained the gentle rolls beside it and rode through the dripping dark until the dull shadowy scar of a fault appeared in the sheer face of Bullhide. That fault lifted him sharply five hundred feet and brought him by quick turns to the canyon's margin. Listening there a little while, he heard nothing of consequence; and for that matter expected nothing. The canyon buried its own sounds and there was only the steady rolling of wind through it. In this sightless night was a trail along the rim which he took with full confidence in his horse and his own ancient knowledge. Eight miles onward he paused, understanding that at this point a trail broke downward by precipitous degrees to the canyon's bottom. This was the first exit. If Luke Daunnt was in a hurry to leave the Bullhide gorge behind him, here was the probable point of departure.

He flattened on the trail, lighted a match and discovered no recent imprint. Rising up then, his mind harked back to that accumulated experience of outlawry. "Better for my purpose," he said quietly to himself, "if they stay in the canyon a while. There they are, with the money of the bank between them, full of jealousy and suspicion. It will work out as it always works out."

So he built a fire, a strong fire, on the very edge of the chasm; and stayed long enough to see its flames ravel up into the sky like a signal flare. Afterwards he mounted and traveled onward, deeper into this avoided and forgotten land, unhurried because he knew there was no need to hurry.

Three miles inside Bullhide, Daunnt and his men had crossed a shallow, evaporating creek that ran down the gorge, and sheltered themselves in a recess bored out by a one-time charging current. Firelight stained the rock walls the color of blood. Yuma the half Navajo sat away from the light, his moon-round cheeks inscrutable; Slash Bill Evans, thin and long and taciturn, crouched on his heels, palms spread against the heat; and Luke Daunnt stood massively upright, bold face bent toward Earl Shaneways, who lay there on the gravel dying.

Shaneways was dying and he knew it. He knew, too, that not one of those other three cared. They watched him indifferently, almost as if they despised him for the delay he caused them — so silently that the ticking of his watch made a distinct sound. His cheeks were lank and drained, his lips curled from the clawing pain of that bullet hole placed in him in the fusillade at Rainwater.

Knees drawn up against his chest, he stared at Luke Daunnt with eyes sprung wide — that full glance of human terror preceding death.

And he said, slowly, between his teeth:

"Do something about it, Luke."

"You're goin'?" grunted Daunnt and showed an interest that was something like a spectator's curiosity.

"Do something about it!" strained Shaneways.

"Nothin' to do," said Daunnt and kicked the fire with a booted toe.

"No, I guess not," said Shaneways and locked his muscles against a long spasm. A wave of pallor passed across his face, a beaded sweat spread over his forehead. "By God, I wish I had the last week back again!"

Slash Bill Evans leaned forward and put two fingers on the dying man's neck, then looked significantly to Daunnt. Shaneways caught the telltale expression and he said bitterly: "I'll die in my own style. Don't try to hurry me."

"What are you regrettin' most?" asked Daunnt with that same strange interest.

"Something — a long time ago," said Shaneways faintly and sank to a seeming stupor. The other three exchanged glances. Daunnt began talking with a stark indifference toward the man flat on the gravel: "He may go next minute or he may hang on for a day. No use waitin' it out."

"Just so," agreed Slash Bill Evans and turned toward Yuma. Yuma only nodded.

"All right," said Daunnt abruptly, "we'll go."

Slash Bill Evans got up and had to bend his neck against the tunnel's top. He was a thin figure throughout and the pointed features had a close, hungry look about them. He caught Daunnt with a swift word: "Wait a minute. The money divides three ways now instead of four."

Daunnt swung and stared. "Yeah," he muttered.

Yuma pulled his stocky body upright, came from the rear of the tunnel. "Divide it here."

"No," contradicted Daunnt, "I'll carry it till we've got more time." But some new thought glimmered in the dull eyes of the man and he cast a swift look at Slash Bill Evans, whose own narrowed glance contained a veiled comprehension. Daunnt said, "Come on, we're losin' time," and started out. Neither he nor Slash Bill Evans looked again at the dying Shaneways. Only Yuma turned at the tunnel's mouth, gazing down with a luminous pity, shaking his head. Shaneways' eyes were open, watching with a clear awareness. Yuma raised one hand, palm turned upward. "So long, Earl," he murmured. All the answer he got was a black and despairing flash of rage. At that, Yuma went out.

"Leave his horse," said Daunnt. "It's no good to us. Now we better bust it harder."

170

They crossed the creek and aimed into the deeper reaches of the gorge. The walls were looming suggestions rather than visible realities, but there was the feel of an increasing height above them and of a widening floor here below. Half a mile onward they crossed the creek again, the water deeper.

"You know this thing pretty well?" inquired Slash Bill.

"So-so," said Daunnt.

"Find a trail and get out of it," said Slash Bill. "It's a trap."

"It's the quickest way into the part of the hills we want to reach," answered Daunnt.

The canyon curled sharply to the left and afterwards took another abrupt turn to the right. They made two more fords of the meandering stream, the water curling higher about the horses' feet. Slash Bill fell to swearing through the utter dark:

"Hell of a lot of water all of a sudden. It was only an inch deep in the lower end. Where's it go to?"

"Sinks in the gravel fast," said Daunnt.

"Look," called the trailing Yuma.

They came around the reverse bend suddenly, and halted. McQuestion's fire leaped against the night, far overhead.

"Posse!" yelled Slash Bill. "I told you this was a trap! Now where's the first trail up the other side? We've got to get out of here!"

Luke Daunnt sat silent, watching the fire until the restless Slash Bill began to grumble afresh. Then Daunnt broke in calmly: "Don't worry. What d'you suppose that fire's there for?"

"Signal to somebody near at hand."

"It's put there for us to see," reflected Daunnt. "To scare us up the other side. Into somebody's gun. We'll keep on as we are. And we'll beat 'em to the end."

Then, hours later, just before the dawn, they came upon a milk-white path of water across the whole width of the canyon — water which beat against the opposite walls, swung and raced along the foot of it.

"Why," grunted Daunnt, surprised, "this thing was only a little crick last summer. Where's the nearest trail out?"

Yuma, long silent, raised a hand and said: "Wait — listen!"

Matt McQuestion left his fire, rode another two miles and arrived at a second trail into the chasm. He went down this and crossed the bottom from west to east, fording the shallow creek; and cruised gently ahead for perhaps a thousand yards until he located the presence of a trail leading out. Once more above the channel of blackness, so deep and so long, he paused to orient himself and to consider. This was sight less pursuit, but he was playing the game out as Luke Daunnt would be playing it and he thought he understood Daunnt's idea; it was a quicker run to the fastnesses of Bullhide Range through the natural corridor of the gorge than via the cut-up land on either side.

"He'll travel fast and try to make it out by daylight," mused the sheriff. "That's not far off. But there is something he forgot to consider, which is the ways of nature. It rained back on Bullhide Peak two days ago."

Once more he put the pony in motion, the contour of the land forcing him back from the rim. It took him, this detour, to a table summit whence he could see the desert sweep eastward vaguely, and from that vantage point he discovered a fire brightly burning out on the flats — one high spire of light plentifully fed. Without much thought over the matter, he knew it was the posse signaling its position. The boys, disobeying instructions, had raced on along the foot slopes of Bullhide in the hope of rejoining him.

"Disappointed not to be in the play," he reflected gently. "And wishin' to see a kill. Luke's heated the blood of a county and the blame is on him. This business is for old sinners like me — and I trust those lads never know what it is to smell the powder of a shell that has knocked the light and the breath out of a human bein'."

Afterwards he traveled more rapidly along the up and down trail, hitting the tricky turns, sharply alert to the lesser pits of Bullhide on either side. The course returned him to the chasm slightly before dawn and so he was stationed on a towering ledge when the sun rose to melt the mist below. Half a mile up the gorge he saw the fugitives; they were then rounding a bend and soon vanished from sight. "Now knowin'," he said to himself, "that it rained two days ago on the upper Bullhide peaks." He sat there while the minutes went by and the day strengthened, thinking that he had seen only three horses; and quite slowly his mild face turned austere as the sense of that fact took hold. "As I figured," he said gently. "Four men went in, but fewer will come out. It is one less to handle." Lifting his gun from the holster he fired thrice into the air, spacing the shots; and then drew clear of the rim, cutting back into the more contorted slopes again.

"Listen," repeated Yuma, the half Navajo.

"Signalin'," muttered Slash Bill Evans and turned on Daunnt with a throttled rage: "I told you to get out of this! By God, we're trapped! We can't go back!"

"No," said Daunnt, "we'll have to chance the water. But we're ahead of 'em. Once across and the trick's done. Only four miles to the clear."

The three wheeled and rode to the margin of that charging stream.

"Never make it," muttered Slash Bill Evans, pointed features more angular than before.

"Three abreast," said Daunnt, "and let the ponies have their own way. The man that falls is gone. Nobody else can help him."

"I don't like it," said Yuma, tonelessly and very quiet.

But the others were sidling into the loose edges of the water and Yuma came forward to his place. Daunnt, nearest the source of the current, turned his horse gingerly and urged him on. The pony advanced, dropped knee-deep and was instantly swayed by the shock of that assaulting force. Slash Bill Evans yelled something that had no meaning, but Daunnt's visage was fixed as iron as the horse beneath him sank deeper, trembled throughout and was shaken off its footing. Instantly animal and rider were whipped about, bobbing like a piece of cork. Daunnt threw both his arms apart and sat crouched, balancing himself. He shot behind Slash Bill, just as Slash Bill's horse reached the safe shelving on the far side. He crouched lower and he spoke to the horse, the sound whipping away in the uproarious water; and afterwards he looked toward Slash Bill and grinned. For he was safe too on the far shore.

But Yuma was not. Yuma cried out, a terrified and arresting cry that caught the instant attention of the others. Yuma's horse had stumbled badly as it gained better footing and Yuma, precariously balanced with feet free from the stirrups, had rolled from the saddle and was wrenched instantly away, hat whirling off into the mill-race current. Yuma's head went under and reappeared twenty yards farther along. Then it disappeared.

Slash Bill turned to Daunnt and reached for his tobacco sack, shaking out a smoke with steady fingers. "Hell of a way to die, Luke."

"No worse than any other," said Daunnt. "We've got to push along. It'll be clear travelin' ahead. They can't get there in front of us."

Slash Bill looked closely at Daunnt, mouth thinning. "Two-way split now instead of three."

"Yeah," said Luke Daunnt and slowly turned his head on Slash Bill. The two of them watched each other carefully, alertly. "Come on," prompted Daunnt, and never moved until his partner rode abreast.

Thus, side by side, they advanced through

the flooding light of another day. The narrowest of the canyon was behind. Ahead, the great walls began to spread and gradually diminish in height; and the floor beneath them took a distinct upward grade. They went at a moderate gallop, which was the best the jaded horses would do, and they turned another great bend. In front of them, not more than three miles, was the promise of smaller corridors leading off into the secretive recesses of the range. Daunnt suddenly said, "Here's a drink, Bill," and stopped before a little spring bubbling out of the earth. He got down, unhooked his canteen from the saddle horn and knelt to fill it, crouched in such a way as to keep his eyes on Slash Bill Evans, who began an impatient muttering:

"No time to delay, Luke. Those hounds won't tarry none now. Chances are they seen us."

"I've been telling you," answered Daunnt patiently, "that they've got a rough trail. We'll be out of here long before they catch up. Better fill that canteen. It's dry in those hills."

Slash Bill got down reluctantly and brought his canteen forward. Luke Daunnt rose and strolled back to his horse, replacing the canteen and fiddling with the cinch of his saddle. Slash Bill's back was momentarily to Daunnt, but only momentarily, for he wheeled with a quick alarm and half rose. Daunnt, shielded by the horse and still busy with the cinch, drawled on conversationally: "When we're out of this, Bill, we'll make for the Dolomite Peak. It's about ten miles. A thousand places around it to hide in. Couple weeks of that and we drift on out of the country. We did the thing right."

"Yeah," muttered Slash Bill, and looked back to the water hole. Over his shoulder he said: "I don't mind the kid Malloy so much. But Shaneways and Yuma — they traveled a long time with us."

"Why worry?" countered Luke Daunnt indifferently. "There's got to be an end sometime for all of us."

"Yeah," grunted Slash Bill, rising to his full gangling height. "Yeah, I guess so. We'll divide the pot here, Luke. Might have to separate up there in the hills."

Daunnt frowned, shook his head. "This ain't the place to do it. We're wastin' the good minutes."

Slash Bill was, of a sudden, formidably stubborn. "What'd you make this stop for?"

"Water, you fool."

"No, I don't think so," rapped out Bill. "Look here, Luke. There ain't any charity between us. You'd shed no tears when the other boys went. You'd shed no tears if I went. You stopped for a chance at me. Only, I didn't turn my back long enough."

"I never knew you to have nerves before," said Luke, calm and cold.

"Nerves be damned! I see a play when it comes. You meant one for here. I figured that out when Yuma went down the crick. So we'll split the pot now."

"We're wastin' time," warned Luke and leaned his big body against the horse. That horse was between the two and all that Daunnt presented to his partner was his head and feet. Arms and torso were hidden. Slash Bill appeared to realize this tardily, and with the realization a harder flash of light sprang out of his eyes. Immediately he began a long striding for his horse. Daunnt said idly: "We're spotted. Somebody's standin' on the rim."

Slash Bill stopped dead and his attention went around, traveling upward. At that a tidal sweep of brutality caught and shook Luke Daunnt's features. Lips and nose thinned, showed pale. His arm whipped over the saddle, gun rising with it. He grinned barrenly into Slash Bill's back-whipping face.

"You asked for it," said Luke, and fired once. Slash Bill staggered back on his heels. A small sound issued from his opened mouth, the whole set of his visage shifted and lost comprehension; and then he fell and was dead.

Luke Daunnt looked at the man over the interminable moments, the grin fading and the tautness of his expression slowly shifting again to that dogged, heavy calm. Presently his head came about and he swept the rim with a long, long glance while the echo of the shot beat away and died in the depths of the gorge. With its final note, a sense of haste seemed to hit him, for he moved impetuously around the horse, threw himself into the saddle and spurred off.

The canyon's floor kept spreading until it was a contained valley between the diminishing rims. Summer's yellow grass carpeted this bottom all the way forward to a finger of the forest that came down from the heights to divide the canyon's source into two lesser ravines. One curled eastward — that way leading out to the desert. The other swooped back into the fastnesses of Bullhide Range. Luke Daunnt gave the matter no thought, but aimed toward the latter course. The land began rolling upward more definitely and he drew abreast the tip of the tree belt and at once bent against his saddle to play the pony for as much as it would give. Now in a distinct runway, with timber to either side of him and a rolling summit ahead, he flashed the full force of those predatory eyes all about. The slopes of the summit turned increasingly severe and the pony faltered; thus at a walk he arrived at the top — and wrenched down on the reins, almost throwing the horse to its knees.

Matt McQuestion stood twenty yards away, rifle cradled and the long body motionless under the light. The sheriff's words rippled through that brief interval of silence with an odd, singsong melody:

"Raise your hands, Luke."

Luke Daunnt cried, "McQuestion — how — !" And then he fell out of the saddle and hauled the shivering horse around to shield him, at once clawing for his revolver. Mc-Question's words came on, clear and pointed:

"Too bad, Luke, too bad." One single report cracked the stillness of the morning. Daunnt's horse winced and shuddered and bucked wildly away, collapsing on the very margin of the timber. Exposed, a guttural rage in his throat, Luke Daunnt began a wild firing at the immovable target in front of him. He cried out mightily, "McQuestion, you're a tricky hound!" The sharper, flatter crash of the sheriff's rifle strangled the rest of the sentence in Luke Daunnt's throat. The renegade's bones seemed to shatter at the joints. His weapon fell, he buckled at the knees and his heavy head swept forward and down, to carry the rest of him to the earth all of a sudden.

Watching with a distant aloofness, McQuestion saw the man's blackened fingers stretch out toward the revolver, halt and relax.

The sheriff studied that prone figure while the reverberations sailed away and made undulating echoes far up along the secretive alleys of the range; and his faded eyes slowly lost the set coldness they had maintained all through his weary chase. Thoughtful, a little wistful, he inclined the fine, spare face as if he were praying.

"Same story," he mused, "played out to the same end. Sinners like Luke and me have lived beyond our time — but Luke never knew it."

Slowly, for he felt the stiffness and the weariness coming upon him now, he knelt down and built a little fire and cooked his coffee in the tomato can, waiting for the posse to come up on the heels of the firing.

Wild Enough

Henry Horn complained: "What am I to guess?"

"Keep Rand under key for thirty-six hours," said Miles Anderson. "That is all."

"I'd like to be in on it."

"Why do you think I brought him here at three o'clock in the morning? I want him sunk from sight for thirty-six hours."

Three blue globes slightly diffused the frigid, muddy gloom of the cell corridor and the metallic color of this winter night cut black squares through the windows. A drunk in the vags' cell threshed his body across a wooden floor screaming; January's wicked prairie wind rushed sibilantly along the outer edges of the building. Miles Anderson stood there, laying his will against the sheriff's will in silence, the raised collar of his fleece-lined coat rubbing the solid edges of a purely western face, somewhat hawkish, somewhat hungry, and very smooth. He was young, with the dower of free-running blood apparent in him, but these mealy jail shadows crept into the softer joinings of his features and obliterated them and

183

left only an intractable changelessness in high relief.

Henry Horn, faintly shivering from the memory of the warm bed Miles Anderson had summoned him from, stared at Rand locked behind the bars. Rand, never speaking, let his eyes express his rage.

"All right," sighed Henry Horn, and turned down the stairs into his office. A small night light shed a wan halo on barren walls and barren furniture; the blued metal of half a dozen racked rifles reflected faint parallel streaks of glow. Henry Horn laid an old, tired glance on Anderson. "It's on the square or you wouldn't ask it, but I want some of this."

Miles Anderson pulled on his gloves. "I'm using Rand's cabin up in the pines, but I can't use Rand. Such as the story may be, you'll get it. I'm a pretty patient waiter, Henry. Is that enough?"

Henry Horn said: "You can be rough and tough when you're so inclined, Miles."

"Sometimes we come to a corner that needs turning. Tom Cherburg was the best friend I ever had. All right, Henry."

Miles Anderson passed into that peculiarly brittle coldness presaging snow; and in fact there were flakes in this bitter wind drumming Pendleton's housetops and plucking its eerie tones from the telephone wires. The town was asleep at this hour and the street lamps marched along the blankness of wall and window with an indescribably lonely effect. It was easy, in this situation, to think of the land as it really was — primeval solitude returning to claim its own, hovering over a little manmade compound that had no validity after dark. Towns died and men died; the ancient hills remained. Head down, shoulders swinging impatiently against the wind, he cut diagonally across the intersection for the hotel. "Some things don't change," he said, half aloud.

The hum of mufflers fled with the wind and two closed cars slid off the residential hill and across the bridge, to halt at the hotel's curb. Half a block removed, he saw a mixed party get out and run into shelter, a few high-pitched words whipping on. As he came up he noticed that one of the cars belonged to Sam Medellon, cattleman of his own age, from the LaGrande side of the Blues; when he entered the lobby he suddenly confronted them. And for some reason or other his entrance turned all their sleepy, curious eyes his way. Sam Medellon, a roan-headed man as temperamental as electricity, said:

"Why didn't you tell me you were in town? Listen, people, this is Miles Anderson, of Y Cross."

He made no effort to remember the names Medellon spoke. They were, he guessed, the usual high-powered young people up from Portland on a week-end trip and now showing the wear and tear of wasted hours. They had been drinking, but the drink was wearing off and all that held them together was the deeply ingrained manners of their kind. The men's faces had a wooden oiliness of fatigue, a faint blueness of jaw and eye-socket; as for the women, they were on wire edge, talking in tones pitched too high and too loose. They were rather vivid girls, wraps thrown back from bare, powdered shoulders and from evening dresses only meant to show the frank modeling of their bodies. Aloof and indifferent, he picked up Medellon's talk again.

". . . Judith Steele. This may interest you, Miss Steele. Miles runs Y Cross, which your grandfather owned in his lifetime. The party's from San Francisco, Miles. Miss Steele's marrying Lew Drummond — no, this one — tomorrow night. A little sentiment. She wants to marry in the town her family sprung from."

Disinterest fell from him. She stood slightly apart from the group; consciously or unconsciously, he didn't know, but the effect was at once gripping. The late hours and the fast pace had done nothing to her; she was somehow fresh and turbulent beneath a surface as hard as onyx, as smooth as glass. Thick copper hair ran back from a broad brow and pale temples, and in the strange levelness of her eyes — disturbing a long-forgotten memory in him — was a light that burned as clear and still as a candle's glow in a quiet room. It was cool, speculative — very deliberate in intent; it was like a call from a great distance. The gown she wore rose in close, yellow-gold curves from narrow hips to thin straps across erect, faintly arrogant shoulders.

"Click," said a limp girl in a red dress, sleepily.

A man — it was Lew Drummond — moved toward Judith Steele and took her arm, the trace of possession there. "Tomorrow's another day," he said. "Or today is."

They straggled up the stairs, wearily complaining of the steps. The limp girl now murmured: "Where's chivalry? Push me up, somebody." Miles Anderson swung sharp on his heels and went to the door. But Sam Medellon called out, "I want to see you after breakfast, Miles," and he turned and got one more glance at Judith Steele. She was at the stair landing, poised against the newel post and looking down at him with that same proud, translucent wonder. The girl in the red dress laughed and said "Click" again and put a careless arm around Lew Drummond's shoulders. "You better marry that woman, Lew, before you lose her. This is the country of the barbarian, and it's a Steele tradition. Being carried off, I mean. Oh, torture!"

Eyes and forehead and a still intensity along clear brows. Miles Anderson went out to the bitter street and to his own car at the curb with this in his mind. He drove down Court Street, passed the rodeo grounds and swung into the Old Oregon Trail, heading east. Beyond the limits of town the wind, no longer baffled, hurled itself savagely on the car and steering became difficult. It was then definitely snowing and all the flat land of the reservation was overwhelmed by a curdled black. Presently he reached the foot of the Blues and began a long circling that took him higher and higher into the desolation of this January night. A filling station's lonely beam glimmered abreast and soon died behind the thickening flurry. He remembered then. Out of his boyhood recollections marched the face of old Guerdon Steele, her grandfather. That full-living, piratical man had had the same unquenchable and lusty flame in his eyes, the same air of rugged independence.

Near the summit, fifteen miles from Pendleton and buried in the pines, Miles Anderson ran the car from the road, opened the radiator drain and walked away. He struck a side trail and went a half mile along it, as far as the black outline of a cabin squatted faintly against lesser black. At this point his thinking ran wholly into sensory impressions and he halted there with a taut, hard interest controlling him, facing Rand's cabin and all that Rand's cabin meant in the next thirty-six hours. Feet slipping in the fresh snow, he circled the place, pressed a back door open and entered a thick, sightless silence.

The girl in the red dress pulled that dress over her head and heard it rip, and said "Damn!" with a faint, weary petulance. "Is there no heat in this room, Carol? Ring for extra blankets. I haven't been warm since we got off the train."

Her roommate, bundled in a quilted robe, bowed an ash-blond head over a cigarette. "I had planned," she said, "to be a very striking bridesmaid, walking up the cathedral aisle with half San Francisco looking on. This last-minute rush to the wilderness leaves me utterly flat." She turned and looked at the other out of alert eyes. "Tell me, my dear Watson, why a girl with the most impressive wedding of the Christian era in prospect should suddenly junk it and run a thousand miles to be married before some local justice of the peace."

"She said she hated a wedding that was a cross between a Roman spectacle and a Stanford-California football game. She said she wanted to be married in the town her grandfather practically put together in his spare moments. The man must have been a barbarian. Where else could Judith have gotten the nerves of a parachute jumper and that utterly outrageous energy?"

"I have a different answer," said the ash-blond. "She doesn't want much of an audience to this bargain — because she's not so sold on the bargain."

"How charitable we are! Listen, darling. Judith's entirely too primitive to look at marriage as something to fill in an idle day."

"Well, there's something in that beautiful head and it isn't all romance. On occasion she can be brutally realistic. I know the signs. When she's restless she gets on a train. Here we are, aren't we?"

At four that afternoon, twelve hours later, another premature night was closing down. The wind had stopped and the snow, falling straight and solid and continuous, blanketed the earth and all the earth's sounds, its ceaseless screen isolating the cabin. Beyond, nothing much could be identified except trees dimly banked against a failing light. Miles Anderson had only a moment ago lighted the lamp and was in the act of stoking the kitchen stove when the knock drummed the front door; whirling about, nerves cocked, he saw the door swing and Judith Steele swiftly enter.

When her eyes found him he knew that whatever she might have expected here she had not expected him. The quick, surprised glance dwelt on him and a faint relief came and passed, leaving remote amusement behind. Her talk was full-noted, unhurried, without waste.

"I ran out of gas half a mile down the main highway. Pendleton seemed a million light years away until I discovered the telephone wire leading in here."

A short spasm of cold shook her; snow particles sparkled with silver brilliance against the bronze hair showing beneath a brimless hat's edges. The weather had bitten mercilessly through her sheer clothes, had turned her face somehow bleak. Miles Anderson nodded back to the kitchen fire. "You had better get in there."

Some thought indefinably changed the color of her eyes, and her head tipped on him, and he felt himself being analyzed for his danger with an utter realism. Held in that judging survey, he saw her waiting for the answer, plainly without much fear or without much hope. It vaguely irritated him — the penetrating power of that wisdom which seemed so sure and had so little faith — and he said, rather ironically:

"You'll have to take your chances. But I suppose that's part of your equipment."

She turned into the kitchen and sat down and removed her shoes. Her voice came back to him on an even, modulated note: "This was all impulse. It came to me that I wanted to see the ranch Grandfather started from. I was very young when I left and all I have of him are the family reports. So I left Pendleton without a word."

Her candid glance touched him again; the fire spread a richer coloring across cheeks from which all definite emotion had subsided. But, passing around to chuck more wood into the stove, he thought some inner defense had fallen before ease. Abruptly it was full night outside, with the snow ticking the window panes and an odd rumor coming across the opaque dark. It turned him motionlessly attentive; and then he went hurriedly along the windows to draw the burlap curtains together. He brought the lamp to the kitchen and afterwards rummaged Rand's cupboard.

The girl said: "Your remark about my equipment stung a little. Am I that transparent?"

"I'm sorry."

Her answer was almost curt: "Don't say things you don't mean. But if you mean them, stick by them. Is this part of the ranch?"

"No, we're both visitors here tonight."

"Will I be able to thank the host?"'

"I doubt it."

Change stirred the dreaming quiet of her face. "You were waiting for somebody, and not in friendliness. Sam Medellon says you can be tiger as well as gentleman. Your face was hard and bitter. It is trying to be smooth now, without luck. If I have disarranged a scene I'm truly sorry."

Her long sheer-modeled legs extended frankly toward the stove; the room's drowsiness further softened the alive audacity of that curved body. Yet her slanting glance contained the same acute and introspective wonder. "They say my grandfather had a cat's perceptions for trouble. I'm like him. I may not know, but I feel. My life's been wholly that — a feeling without direction."

"Your grandfather would also have apologized for interrupting a scene. But if it looked interesting he would have asked a part. He never liked being a spectator. It was, as far as he was concerned, a black-and-white world."

"There were no complexities in his days," she observed gently.

Rand's cupboard yielded a lump of bacon, a stiff sheet of corn bread and a can of coffee. Miles Anderson sliced the bacon into the frying pan and slid it across the stove. He filled the coffee-pot from the water bucket; laid two pie tins and two crock cups on the table. "What's complex in your days?"

He heard then the first break in her self-assurance, the first stir of rebellion. "Why am I here in this cabin? Why did I come back to a land I never really remembered?"

"I've heard that people get stage fright on the eve of a wedding."

"Biology?" she said. The flush deepened and he saw the inner resources of this girl turn vigorous. "I'd not be afraid of that," she said. "I'm not shy. How could I be, educated with the set you saw in the hotel lobby? There's no vinegar in me, Miles. I'm — I'm rather humanly robust in my desires." The little silence came, accenting that remark. She watched him obliquely, and added: "You saw it when you first looked at me."

He said, brutally direct: "You've waited too long for marriage."

"Perhaps," she agreed. "Perhaps." Silence and reflection again. It was clearer and clearer to him that below the false quiet a turbulent energy lay unexpressed, without means of expression. "But that isn't all, Miles. There's got to be something behind the giving, something received for girlhood lost. Look." She sat straight, suddenly demanding, suddenly afire. She lifted her two arms and the curve of shoulder and breast strengthened beneath her dress. "Haven't I strong bones and muscles? What am I for? Not just surrender." A great square engagement solitaire flashed out a smoky brilliance.

He said: "If these are your thoughts one day before the wedding, you're marrying the wrong man."

"The torch scene," she said, matter-of-fact, "wasn't deliberate."

"Of course not. But you run a risk."

She said, speculatively, "Do I?" She shook her head. "My training has been nothing if not practical. For what it may be worth, I know when a man goes savage."

He took off his coat and hung it on a nail, and when he swung around he found her eyes set on the gun tucked inside his trousers band. A thread of excitement flashed out; that deliberate intentness bore on him again. They fell to the plain meal.

"You've asked me almost no questions," she mused.

"When you've made up your mind you'll tell me."

"Well, what could be done?"

He pointed to the telephone on the wall. "The road's blocked now, but your man could get here by midnight with horses."

"Let's think of another way. Lew wouldn't thank me for putting him to that much physical effort."

"The snow plows will open the road by morning. I can find you a little gas from my car then."

She said, gently: "Would you mind?"

"No. The risk is yours, not mine."

"Reprieve," she murmured.

Miles Anderson rose, but the girl said, "Let me," and moved around the table. She filled a pan with water, placed it on the stove to heat. Her hand dipped into the water and the great solitaire exploded sudden shafts of light. Judith Steele looked thoughtfully at it and slipped it off her finger to the table; and, seeing those supple, graceful hands plain and unpossessed before him, Miles Anderson turned into the front room with shock somersaulting violently through him.

There was a tholepin hanging beside the door latch, and he seated it; there was a rifle canted against the wall, and he lifted that and opened the magazine. He emptied the magazine, carried the gun to the kitchen. Presently the water was hot and Judith Steele fell to the dishes. Idle, he watched her lips soften and firm up and soften again while her thinking isolated her. The lustrous head rose and her eyes, glowing, looked through him and beyond him.

He said heavily, "You're marrying the wrong man," and broke off. The wall phone struck one faint tone preliminary to a long, tinny alarm. Judith Steele straightened, swift shadow turning more somber the actual, urgent beauty of her features. Miles Anderson took down the receiver, remaining silent until he heard Henry Horn's prosaic voice, looping up and down eighteen miles of storm-sagged wire, arrive noncommittally.

"There?"

"Yes."

"There's a half million dollars' worth of Frisco luxury floatin' around the hills in silk stockin's and a light car that won't shed an ounce of snow. Seen her?"

"No."

"She left without aye, yes or no. Filling-station man at summit saw her pass east. Before dark. That's all. You sure you ain't seen her?"

"No."

"Well, she'll sure freeze if she's stalled on the road. This Drummond's been breathin' down my neck for three hours."

There was a long pause. Miles Anderson

studied the wall, making stray lines on it with a thumb nail. He said: "I wouldn't worry — until morning."

Henry Horn's grunt was distinct. "Why didn't you say so?" He hung up.

"Thank you," murmured the girl, "for the interlude."

"Tomorrow's the day you get married."

"Miles," she demanded, "what do you think of me?"

"Why?"

"Never mind."

She sat on the bunk, slender legs tucked under, her back against the wall in the attitude of repose; but there was no repose inside the lax symmetry of that body, no calm. The wide and even eyes were sultry with rebellion, and underneath the roundness of shoulder and breasts that sense of a turgid energy strengthened. He looked once, and then away, speaking through his pipe smoke:

"Guerdon Steele walked into this country penniless and when he died he left a million dollars that your father took to Frisco to invest and that you, in your turn, can't possibly spend. Guerdon never gave a damn about money. He sowed his dollars in the streets of Pendleton when he was drunk. When he was sober he laughed about it. He liked living — he liked what he could smell and see and feel. He never rode a gentle horse, he never sat in a chair when he could squat on his heels. He trailed a horse thief eight hundred miles, found three thieves waiting for him — and left all three dead right there.

"When his own turn came to die he was lord of eighty thousand owned acres and his only regret was that he knew his son hated the place and wouldn't keep it. So he arranged for eight Umatilla Indians to come after he was dead and carry him away on a travois and bury him after dark and burn a fire on the grave so all trace of it would be lost. Some of the things he did weren't pretty, but none of them was small. He was a sort of savage, never knowing a mild moment, never wanting to. Good luck or bad luck didn't matter. It was the game that counted and it had to be lively. There were others in the land like him, but I think the pattern's busted now."

Judith Steele laced her fingers together. "No," she whispered. "Not altogether broken." And she studied him with a flickering strangeness.

"That's your bed," he said, and stood up. Rising, she watched him take the top blanket and walk to the kitchen.

What woke him was the muted threshing of horses' feet in the thick snow, the echoes penetrating that otherwise stillness of the buried hills. The notice brought him instantly up from his blanket on the floor, for all his sleeping had been fitful, contingent on the certain knowledge that they would come before full day. Faint, gray light swirled through the rooms and when he slid the curtains of the kitchen window aside he looked out upon a cheerlessly violet world. He saw nothing of them then; only heard a brief and cautious call run from the trees:

"Rand."

He passed to the front room, drew the tholepin from the door latch; he lighted the lamp and let his fingers brush the top of the gun aside his waistband. And then he looked down at Judith Steele, curled child-like beneath the quilts, the copper hair shaken around sleep-flushed temples. He had meant to waken her, but she was already awake and watching him quietly, and he thought then that she realized there was trouble. Saying nothing, he cut a path toward the kitchen with his hand and turned away, hearing her slip quickly to the kitchen. Afterwards he parted the living-room window curtains and surveyed the narrow clearing again.

Two shadows emerged from the trees, each rider and horse making a welded shape against that curt, chilly twilight. Rand's name was spoken more insistently; the horses stumbled on through the drifts and halted. A voice arrived: "Get on — get on." In another moment they had circled the house and stopped by the front door, seeming to wait. Judith whispered from the kitchen, "All right, I'm dressed," and at that Miles Anderson retreated from the lamp and faced a suddenly opening door across the width of the room.

Abe LeBold came in first, his big palm extended, the fingers splayed. One curl of jet, dense hair crept down from the brim of a sleet-caked hat and struck an instant air of recklessness across a face extremely broad and blunt. Big jaws shelved out from flat neck hinges and a kind of animal health simmered in eyes as unwinkingly watchful as those of a wolf. Behind a shoulder of this vast man stood the henchman Forgan, vertical lines of his shad cheeks gray with changeless evil, protected as always behind the physical greatness of LeBold. Both men stopped and stared over the lamp — for that one moment sightless because of the long night in their eyes. Forgan kicked the door shut and LeBold said: "We're late, Rand. How about some coffee?"

Miles Anderson said, inexpressibly soft: "Coffee, Judith."

The rigors of shock seized both. Forgan took one sideward step and lifted an arm, fingers hanging limply from the wrist in a way that reminded Anderson of a setter come to point. But Abe LeBold, hearing what he could not yet see, was a dark statue strained by the lamplight's yellow. Then Miles Anderson saw recognition color his contracting pupils. LeBold's first talk was quick and cautious and hard:

"Stand fast, Forgan."

"You'll get the coffee," said Miles Anderson.

LeBold's glance raced down Miles Anderson and discovered the gun; it lifted over Anderson and found the girl; and it returned to Anderson, narrow and greedy for facts. He murmured out of lips motionlessly apart: "Where's Rand?"

"I couldn't use Rand."

"It ain't clear."

"I tapped Rand's wire and heard you call him day before yesterday. I know the location of every campfire you made from Y Cross to Canada, from Canada back to Y Cross. Five of my men have had you in sight between sundown ever since the twenty-eighth day of November. Rand is your supply agent. I knew that, so I got rid of him."

"A set trap," breathed LeBold. "So where's the men now — where's Henry Horn?"

"No. I tally my own sheep. Didn't you know it?"

"Cold turkey?"

"Not quite cold. You and your mongrel have got guns. You're faced this way. That's better than being faced the other way — like Tom Cherburg was."

Thin irony relieved LeBold's singing phrases: "Find twelve men to agree on that. And what've you got to make sure?"

"Think again. Cherburg left my ranch and went straight to Lobo Creek. That's where we found him, with his face in the water and a bullet through his head. You were on Lobo Creek. Nobody else was, that week. If it isn't enough, you've been prowling the edges of my range for a year. If that isn't enough, you ran for Canada after he was killed."

"Make it stick in court."

"Think again," urged Miles Anderson. He was there in the kitchen doorway, torso and shoulders and head filling it while the brief words ran into the hush like liquid across glass.

"It'll never reach trial," said LeBold. "I know what law is."

"You get a break," said Miles Anderson. "Judith, there's wood outside in the shed."

The door behind him opened and a cold wind gushed on his neck. The door closed.

"You're pretty smooth, Miles," LeBold muttered. "But I think I'll give you my gun and take a jury. I've done it before — and

203

walked the streets of Pendleton a free man. It's the wrong year for a shoot-out."

"It's the same — this year or fifty years ago. As long as grass grows and cattle run. Some things don't change. Tom Cherburg was a friend of mine."

LeBold said, evenly, "Your girl's in the doorway." But that was fake and Miles Anderson knew it from the pure shafts of yellow rage pouring through LeBold's heavy eyes. The man's shoulders rippled with the exertion that sent his arm down and forward and up; and the stunning detonation smashed the too-small space of the rooms and seemed to rend apart the rafter joints. It was one fragment of action smeared into another, nothing clear, nothing distinct. Above LeBold's vest points and below the girth of his neck lay the plain target of his chest, and into it Miles Anderson, without remorse, flung his bullet. Forgan screamed, fired wild, and the lamp flame danced and died in that bedlam, and the smoky, acrid silence came pulsing back to the room.

The scene Anderson saw then was like a moving film whose central pieces had been cut to speed the finish, which was of LeBold lying dead beneath the table and Forgan creeping toward the door, dragging a shattered arm beside him. Down somewhere in the trees a strong shout hollowly beat along the bitter air. The back door opened and Judith Steele ran in, crowding past Anderson and flattening herself against the living-room wall.

Forgan tried to open the front door and failed; and the shouting was then directly in front of the cabin. Forgan said, "Cherburg was your friend and I told LeBold it was bad business gutting him," and cringed away as Henry Horn battered in the door and a clean rectangle of daylight breached the inner gloom. Behind Horn stood a deputy, gun swinging up; behind the deputy stood Lew Drummond, very pale.

But it was Judith Steele that Anderson watched, all the rest of this play turning dim even then in his brain. The lithe body pressed against the wall, shoulder and hip and palm, and along that flat surface her figure made a medallion of wild, vital beauty. The silhouette he saw was without fear, without regret.

Henry Horn said, not surprised: "You said on the phone, not till daylight. Here's daylight. This is it, Miles?"

"I told you the story would come."

"Judith," exclaimed Lew Drummond, and ran at her. "What a miserable thing to put you through!"

"Forgan," said Henry Horn, "what's there about a busted arm to make you shiver so?"

"We can ride one of the horses back to the car," Drummond told the girl.

She went slowly to the bunk and picked up her coat. Drummond held it and Drummond stared at Anderson with a stony unrecognition — a gentleman expressing his deep anger. But Judith suddenly turned to Miles Anderson, all her words rounding out in the hush: "You have made one thing forever impossible for me, Miles," she said.

Miles Anderson plugged a little snow in the radiator and cranked a stone-cold engine to life. He bucked back into the highway and drove between the sheared snow walls, unmindful of the radiator's sudden boiling. At the filling station he stopped for water and eased along the quick turns out of the Blues, soon speeding across the reservation. Pendleton was sloppy with a traffic-churned slush and great pillars had been shoveled in front of the hotel walk, wherein some pragmatic artist had sculptured twin Thunder Birds. Miles Anderson stopped at the desk.

"Miss Steele?"

"Number two-ten — if you can wade through the bridesmaids. They got everything up there but an Episcopal Cathedral. But the fellow bein' married has been takin' some thing for his cold and something's wrong. Tell me? I seen weddings before but they don't begin like this."

He walked thoughtfully to the stairs. A man hustled across the lobby and said: "Wait. Henry Horn phoned in. Henry said Forgan confessed that LeBold had ambushed Tom Cherburg last November and that he'd heard you were looking for him. So he was on his way back to spot you. But it's funny. There's this girl —"

"Not now," said Miles Anderson, and went up. The door of Number 210 was open and a pair of San Francisco girls came out and brushed his elbow and looked up at him with sudden keenness. He stopped on the threshold, saw Lew Drummond in the center of the room speaking to Judith posted at the far windows.

"If it's another weird impulse, I won't stand for it. Eight hours alone with the man! I'm modern, but —" The two girls were coming slowly back along the hall. Judith Steele caught sight of him and her body straightened around and he went in, not sure any more, not confident, feeling Lew Drummond's angry glance eating at him. But then it no longer mattered, for Judith was moving toward him and smiling from half-parted lips. He said, gently, to Drummond:

"It's tough. But sometimes it happens like this."

"Not in eight hours!"

"What's time?" said Miles Anderson. "She's Guerdon Steele's granddaughter."

Drummond was a faint shadow on the edge of his vision, just a shadow growing fainter and fainter behind the high and glowing tumult in Judith's eyes. He said, to her: "What's time?"

She made a little bow, at once gay and reckless. "This is the beginning, Miles. Everything else has been waiting — for both of us."

"Some things never change, Judith."

"Not in eight hours!" complained Lew Drummond.

One of the girls at the doorway caught her breath. "Lew," she said. "Lew, come on out. I could have told you the other night. You're — you're not in that tradition."

When You Carry the Star

Sheriff Henry Linza was taking the evening's ease on the porch of his ranch house, ten miles out of Bonita, when he saw the rider come beating across the prairie; and even at that distance he knew. His face settled a little and he tapped the bowl of his pipe against an arm of his chair as if to signal the end of twilight's long peace. "It's Bob Boatwright," said he to his wife. "Funny how he likes to lug bad news to me."

"How can you tell?" asked Miz Linza.

"He's sittin' all over the saddle," chuckled Linza. "Kind of a St. Vitus' dance catches him when he gets excited." But when Boatwright, marshal of Bonita, came abreast the porch, Linza was quite grave. Indian summer's cloudy beauty lay over the land and it was hard to think of the crimes of men.

"This is bad, Sheriff," said Boatwright. "Will Denton — he's turned wild."

"Will Denton!" exclaimed Miz Linza. "Why, I don't believe it!"

But Henry Linza shook his head slowly and, leaning forward, prompted Boatwright. "As how, Bob?"

"He walked into Neal Sampson's store an hour ago, pulled the gun and asked for the extra money Neal keeps to accommodate ranch hands after the bank closes. Wouldn't been nothin' but ord'nary robbery but Neal is rattled, makes a move toward the counter and gets a bullet in the heart."

"What then?" grunted Linza.

"It was all over in three minutes," said Boatwright. "Last we saw of Denton he was goin' due west into the heat haze. I couldn't get a posse organized so I come here. The boys are shy of Denton's educated rifle, Sheriff."

"I don't believe it," repeated Miz Linza. "Why, he ate supper with us two weeks ago."

"I hated to come here," said Boatwright, "knowin' he was a friend of yours." And after a lengthening silence he spoke again. "What'll you do, Sheriff?"

Linza's head fell thoughtfully forward. Lines curved down from his lip corners into a squarely definite chin, thus creating an aspect of doggedness, of biting into difficulties and hanging on. Without alleviating humor, that cast of jaw and mouth would have seemed unforgiving and almost brutal; but it was Linza's eyes that gave him away. Candidly blue, they mirrored the shrewdness of a full life and the inevitable compassion arising therefrom.

As an observer and dealer in the misdemeanors of men he had grown great without becoming hard; of that splendid line of southwestern peace officers which had left its impress on an unruly land, there was in him always a puzzlement that certain things had to be.

"Go after him," said he, following a long spell of silence.

"Now?" pressed the marshal.

"Mornin's soon enough," replied Henry Linza. "He's got twelve hundred square miles to roam in and one day makes no difference. Light and rest, Bob."

"Thanks, no, I've got to get back," said Boatwright and cantered away into the deepening dusk.

"He sat here on this porch two weeks ago," murmured Miz Linza. "It don't seem possible."

"He was on the border line then," reflected Linza. "I saw it in him. He wasn't the same. He held a little off from me. He was debatin' the jump whilst he ate my beef."

"But what could make him?" pressed Miz Linza.

Linza shook his head. "If anybody knew the answer to that they'd have the answer to all things. Wild blood, a dark thought, a bad day, a tippin' of the balance in a man's mind, a sudden move — and then it's done and never can be undone. One more rider in the wild bunch."

"Your own friend," said Linza.

"Was," agreed Linza, rising. "But it's himself that took the step across the line, and he'd be the first to realize I've got to go after him. Such," and a deepening regret came to his voice, "is the constituted order of things in a mighty queer world. We better turn in, Henrietta. I'll ride early."

It was, in fact, still short of daylight when Henry Linza pulled out from the ranch, riding one horse and leading another. There was a single gun at his hip, a rifle in its boot, a few necessities within the saddlebags, and some quick grub inside the blanket roll tied to the cantle strings. In addition he carried a pair of binoculars. "Can't say when I'll return," he told his wife. "My intention is to take Will peaceably. Knowin' his disposition I dunno if he'll agree. But don't worry."

She had been a peace officer's wife too long to show her concern outwardly. All she did was to touch him gently and return to the porch. A hundred yards off he swung in his saddle and raised his hand as a farewell; it was a comfort to know she'd be there waiting for him to come back.

He swung wide of Bonita and thus when

day fully arrived and a splendid sun swelled through the sky with a rose-red light, he came to a bridge over a dry river bed, crossed it and stood on the edge of his venture. The leagues rolled away to the distance, southwesterly into a horizon unbroken, northwesterly to a line of hills even now beginning to fade behind an autumn haze. Somewhere yonder Will Denton rode. Halting a moment, Linza was summing up as follows: wherever Denton went the need of food and water and rest would inevitably bring him to certain crossroads.

It became a matter of guessing who, out of Denton's many stanch friends in the country ahead, would shelter the man. As for the first crossroad, the dimmed smudge of Joe Waring's ranch in the distance seemed most likely. Hungry and worn, Will Denton would seek that friendly shelter while debating whether to turn to the southern open or to the northern hills. Waring's was the jump-off.

The day's course outlined, he pushed forward at a gait designed to protect both himself and his horses over a continued trail. It was not one that would have overtaken any hurrying fugitives, but Linza, having twenty years' tracking to his credit, knew wild ones seldom if ever retreated in a straight line after the initial dash. They shifted, they halted, they doubled from point to point. As those more gentle, abiding men whose ranks they forsook, outlaws liked home soil best of all.

For the most part it was a trackless, lonely land and as he plodded on, Linza relapsed into the protection of his thoughts. "Punched cattle with him, ate and slep' with him under the stars. Knew him well, but apparently never knew him at all. He was a laughing man. Now he's got a price on his head. Good wine can stand in the keg too long." Beyond noon he camped under a scrub oak.

Afterwards, riding the second horse, he pressed through heat haze as heavy as fog; and around six o'clock he crossed the Waring front yard to find the owner standing in wait for him — a big, broad man with fat cheeks and a pair of blandly observant eyes.

"Saw you comin', Henry," said he. "Glad to have your feet under my table again. Get down."

"Your conscience is clear, I take it," drawled the sheriff cheerfully and allowed an arriving puncher to take his horses away.

"Why shouldn't it be clear?" retorted Waring; and the both of them grinned.

There were punctilios in this matter that had to be observed, a kind of code grown up from the common mingling of honesty and outlawry. Waring, himself straight as a string,

214

was a friend to both the sheriff and Denton. More than that, there was in him a wide streak of sentiment for the under dog, and many men on the dodge had received casual aid from him. But what he knew he kept strictly behind his smiling eyes. Comprehending this, Linza maintained his peace, ate and returned to sit on the porch with a cigar between his teeth while purple dusk deepened and a faintly stirring breeze brought the fragrance of sage across the yard. The thing went even deeper. Waring's sympathy for the under dog might well lead him into getting word out to Denton of his, Henry Linza's, probable course of hunt. So it became a matter of wits, played on either side with a shrewd courtesy.

"You're in no hurry?" said Waring.

"Plenty of time. The world's a wide place."

"Ahuh," drawled Waring and added gently, "one of the boys came back from town last night. Heard about Will Denton from him."

Linza remained silent, wondering whether this were truth or evasion. Waring leaned forward, concern in his words. "You're both friends of mine of long standing. Hard for me to realize you're the man that's got to take Denton's trail. Henry, one of you is going to get hurt."

"I carry the star," said Linza very quietly.

"And not for a million dollars would you

go back on it," muttered Waring. "That damn' fool Denton! He might've known this would happen. You never give up, Henry. I never knew you to give up. And he won't be taken alive. I can tell you that."

"I'll give him every chance to drop his guns," said Linza.

"Why didn't you put a deputy on his trail?"

Linza shook his head slowly. "It would be the same as a lie, Joe. No deputy could catch Will. It takes an old dog full of tricks. It wouldn't even be average honesty for me to send another man out."

"Damn a system that makes this business possible," growled Waring.

Linza sighed a little, remembering Will Denton's recklessly pleasant face as of old. "Maybe — maybe. But bear in mind that Will committed the murder, not the system. I'm turnin' in."

Waring got up, watching the sheriff closely through the shadows. "Listen, you're traveling light. Better let me give you a couple of extra water bags tomorrow."

"Thanks," said Linza casually. "Not a bad idea." And he climbed the stairs to his bedroom. But he didn't immediately roll up for the night; instead, he pulled a chair soundlessly to a window and took station there. A long while afterward he was rewarded by the sight of a rider going off from the barn. In the distance hoofbeats rose and died out. With something like a grim smile on his face, the sheriff abandoned his post and went to bed. "The twelve hundred square miles is cut in half, I think," he mused.

He was away next morning before the mists had risen. Five miles from the ranch he drew in, knowing it was time to make a decision. If he meant to hit for the open land southwesterly it was necessary to swing left at this point; otherwise the hill country beckoned him to turn north. Dwelling on Waring's apparently innocent offer of the water bags and the subsequent rider faring out through the darkness, Linza made up his mind. "Me taking those water bags indicates to Waring I intend to hit the dry trail into the southwest; his messenger would tell Denton that, and Denton would do just the opposite — ride for the hills." Acting on that reasoning, Linza swung somewhat and advanced squarely toward the range of hills shooting tangentially out of the north.

The country began to buckle up and long arroyos led downgrade to a high-bluffed canyon with a silent river idling at the bottom. Linza, roused from his saddle laze, entered the canyon, followed the slanting trail around a bend and found himself in a forlorn, shrunken town hidden from the horizon altogether. This habitation of man appeared to have no purpose and no vitality; and in truth it was but a gateway to the hills and a supply point for the nervous-footed who dodged in and out of sight. Linza, watching all things carefully, knew he had definitely put safe territory behind; the mark of hostility lay on the faces of the few loungers who scanned him with surreptitious, narrow-lidded glances. Pausing to let his horse drink at a stable trough, he considered his surroundings.

"Got to know if Will passed through here. If he didn't, then he's striking into the hills at a point higher up and I've missed his trail somewhere along the line. These folks are his friends, but there is one weak point —"

Turning, he rode farther down the street and dismounted at the general store. Inside the dim, musty place a single occupant's gaunt body stooped over the counter, bald head shining through the half light; when he straightened it was to reveal a face like that of a bloodhound — sad and lined and somehow very honest.

"I'll make out a snack on crackers and cheese, 'Lisha," said the sheriff.

"Love you, Sher'ff," drawled the storekeeper. "What brings you here?"

"Business, 'Lisha."

"Sorry business then," muttered the store-keeper. "It's the only kind we know around these parts."

Linza ate some cheese sandwiches, drank a bottle of warm beer and spoke abruptly: " 'Lisha, did Will Denton pass this way?"

The storekeeper met the sheriff's glance steadily. "No. What's he done?"

"You're the only man who would tell me the truth," grunted Linza. "The only one in this town I could ask or believe."

"My fault," said the storekeeper and appeared unusually sad. "Truth is a bad habit up here."

Linza paid for his lunch, went out and rode away to the north, considering the situation.

If his reasoning was correct, Denton's avoidance of the town meant the six hundred square miles was halved to three hundred; in addition there was a constantly accruing advantage on the sheriff's side, for, as the area of pursuit narrowed, the known waterholes, trails and hideouts became fewer. That night, long after dark, he struck a watering place and inspected its edges by match light. Seeing nothing of value, he suddenly changed his tactics, and under cloak of night left the prairie behind him to rise to the bench and its thin sweeps of timber. Some eyes had always been on him while he was in the open. Putting himself into semi-concealment at once switched the nature of the chase. "The hunted animal," he reflected, "never runs when it figures pursuit is lost. It even circles back to find out where the hunter's gone." Dawn found him in a thicket and there he stayed while the fresh hours ran on to noon. Beside him a definite trail ran up in the direction of the range's crest, and it was while he tarried here that a single rider came cantering down, passed him with eyes fixed on the earth and disappeared. Perhaps an hour later this man returned, riding fast and looking troubled.

"Somebody's nervous," reflected Linza. "Will's got stout friends in these parts. Hell to fall back on a plain hunch but I believe I'll go ahead in this direction."

As he went forward, winding in and out of sloping meadows interspersed with yellow-dusted pines, the ever present attitude of watchfulness continued to deepen. Like some hound in game country, he was keening for a scent he knew ought to be there. Tracks led him onward, passed through bands of cattle and were lost. After the second such happening, Linza left the trail and began to climb in a semicircular manner that around sundown brought him to the edge of a meadow in which a gray cabin sat remote and serene. A brown dog sprawled in the dirt; there was a half-masked lean-to behind the cabin sheltering some implements, and over at the far edge of the meadow an ewe-necked horse grazed. Inside the cabin a woman passed and repassed the door aperture. "Apparently no visitors," said Linza, and went forward.

Instantly the brown dog sprang up snarling and immediately afterward a tall man in a red undershirt strode from the house and took a stand in the yard with a cradled rifle.

Linza rode up.

"Long day behind," said he, amiably. "Could I put up here?"

"You're Linza?" said the man.

"That's right."

"No room fer you in my cabin, sir."

Linza's eyes betrayed a gleam of humor but he said quietly: "Fair answer. I'll roll my blankets up yonder."

"Go beyond my fences afore you do," stated the man.

Linza nodded and rode around the cabin. Two hundred yards on he came to a gate and passed through it. Trees shut off sight of the cabin but he was strongly aroused now and interested in the squatter's subsequent actions. So, a few hundred yards farther ahead, he quartered to the top of a small butte commanding the meadow. The man was not to be seen and Linza, about to retreat, had some oddity tick his mind. Looking more closely, he discovered what he had not observed before and what certainly had been missing at the time he went by the house — a string of white clothes hung on a clothesline.

"It ain't Monday," observed Linza. "And it seems odd the lady would wash near supper time."

Watching for a moment, he finally turned down the butte and continued through the trees. "Will would have glasses and he'd see that washin'," he reflected. "It's a signal to him. Arranged for." It was then dark, a clear cold violet giving way to velvet blackness against which the range made a ragged silhouette. One shot banged from the general direction of the squatter's meadow and its echo sailed over the tree tops and died in small ricocheting fragments. The sound of that gun, primitive and lawless in effect, seemed to defy Henry Linza openly, to taunt and challenge him, and finally to bring him to a decision.

"I'm tradin' on Will's weakness," he muttered. "God knows it's hard enough to have friend set against friend without that. But I'd trade on the weakness of any other and I will not make exceptions. Will, damn you, don't fall into this trap."

Linza moved rapidly toward a depression of the burn, dismounted and picketed his ponies fifty feet apart to keep them from fouling each other. He let the saddle remain on the ridden beast, but he unrolled his blanket beside a protecting deadfall and laid his rifle by it. Going on a distance, he built up a small fire, retreated to the log and ate a pair of cold biscuits.

Not far off, something snapped. A taut, husky voice struck through the shadows.

"Henry — that you?"

Linza swore under his breath. One faint, friendly hope died. "Will, why in hell did you come?"

"You're too old a codger to be buildin' fires for nothin' in country like this. I saw the blaze and I knew you wanted to see me. Well, here I am."

"So I figured," replied Linza, keeping below the log. "Wanted to see you all right, but I had a mite of hope you'd stay away. It's hard business, Will."

Denton's voice was increasingly cold. "Listen — get off my trail. When I heard you was the one after me I knew it had to be a showdown sooner or later. But I'm tellin' you, I'll not be took. Not by you nor anybody else. Get off my trail and keep off it!"

Linza shook his head. This was the inevitable way. Some odd thing happened to a man when he turned killer. Some suppressed fire

223

flamed and would not die. Will Denton was only playing out an old, old story; he had turned wolf. But still the sheriff had his say.

"Give up, Will. Maybe a good lawyer could make out a case for you. Consider a life sentence with the even chance of a pardon some years later. Put down and come forward."

Denton's reply was almost a snarl. "Not me — never!"

"Think of this," urged Linza. "What's left for you now? You'll never sleep sound again. For the rest of your life you'll be ridin' the edges, wishin' to come in and afraid to. Come on, give up."

"You'd make a fine parson," jeered Denton, and the sheriff heard the man's teeth snap, heard the sudden inrush of breath. "I'm on my own hook. I'm not comin' in. Go on back. Get off my trail. I know you and I know myself. If we meet, somebody's goin' to die."

"You know I can't quit," said Henry Linza.

Denton fell silent a moment. Presently he said: "All right, Mister Linza. You've had your warnin'. Expect no consideration from me when we collide. Don't figure friendship will count for anything at all. It won't. If I see you again I won't call out. I'll kill you."

Linza shouted, "You everlastin' fool!"

A single gunshot burst into the night and soared along the slope. Linza's near horse winced, expelled a great gust of air and fell in his tracks. "Keep your head low, Linza!" roared Denton, and there followed a crunching of boot heels across the burn. Linza rose from the log and stared at the blank pall in front of him. Presently he heard Denton's pony struggling up the mountain trail; then the sound of that died.

He crawled to the dead horse, unfastened the gear, and afterward saddled the second animal. Rolling up his blanket roll and tying it, he mounted and waited another long interval with his ear pressed against the night breeze. Far up the side of the range a shot broke out, seeming to be both a challenge and a defiance. When he heard it, Linza went across the burn, entered the trail and began to climb.

"No consideration now," he muttered. "This is a man hunt. And if he thinks he's put me afoot he'll be a mite careless."

The trail wound interminably through the dismal reaches of the night.

Occasionally Linza paused, but never for long, and always the cold, unrelenting thoughts of the hunter plagued him, and the stealth and wariness of the hunter kept him on guard. Sometime after midnight he oriented himself on a dome atop the world, withdrew to a thicket and rolled up for a short sleep. There was the faint smell of wood smoke in the wind.

When he rose the ravines of the range below were brimful of fog that moved like sluggish lake water. Kindling a cautious fire, he boiled coffee and considered it a breakfast.

The strategic importance of his location became more apparent when, after a chill and dismal two hours of waiting, the fog dissipated before sunlight coming across the range in flashing banners that outlined all the tugged angles of the hills boldly. From his station he looked away to lesser ridge tops, to sprawling glens, to the various trails and their intersections; and it was while his patient glance ran from one trail to another that a movement in a corner of his vision caused him to swing slightly and catch sight of a solitary rider slipping from the trees, momentarily pausing in full sight, and disappearing again. He was gone before Linza could get his glasses focused.

Linza lost no time in mounting and running down the slope of the knob he had been posted on — unavoidably exposing himself as he did so. He reached the still dew-damp shelter of the lower pines, struck a runway fresh with the mark of deer tracks and the plantigrade print of bear, and followed it faithfully until he presently arrived at a division point. One fork led descendingly to that crossing where he had seen the man; the other continued along the spine of the ridge.

Wishing to keep his tactical advantage, Linza accepted the latter way and fought through a stiffly resisting accumulation of brush before coming to a fairer path. Traveling faster and all the while sharply watching for the unexpected, he reached, about twenty minutes later, the junction point of his route and another laboring up from the depths of a canyon; and he barely had time to sink into the sheltering brush when the man he was stalking came into sight along the lower trail. Linza cursed silently. It was not Denton.

"Mistake," he muttered. "And could have been damn near fatal to me. Am I bein' towed around the landscape for Will to find?"

The thought stiffened him. He retreated deeper into the brush, scanning one narrow vista and another. Meanwhile the rider came out of the canyon, cut across Linza's vision and disappeared, to reappear momentarily between two great pines at another quarter of the forest.

"Something in that," thought Linza, the hunter's instinct beginning to flow hotter in him. He hauled himself around until he discovered a way of bearing down in the direction of the man. Five minutes later, though hardly more than four hundred feet in distance, the trees ran out upon another meadow. There was a cabin built against a rocky bluff in front of which the rider was then dismounting. Smoke curled from a chimney, but other than that it seemed innocent of trouble. Linza dropped from his horse and crawled to a better vantage point.

The man had left his horse standing beside the cabin, reins down and saddle on. Meanwhile he had slouched forward to a patch of sunshine. Squatting there on his heels, he tapered off a cigarette, lit it and seemed to warm himself leisurely. But at every third or fourth drag of smoke his head made a swift half circle, snapped around and made another.

A moment later, in defiance to his attitude of indolence, the man rose abruptly and strode for an ax standing beside a chopping block. Lifting it, he brought it down, one stroke after another, in rhythmic attacks that sent long ringing waves of sound through the still air. Linza swore to himself, hitched his body a little more forward and turned his glance to that corner of the meadow where the trail entered.

"Something in that," he muttered.

Down the trail was the softly indistinct "clop-clop" of a horse approaching at the canter. The ax strokes ceased and then Will Denton, riding light and alert and casting a continually revolving inspection to all sides, came into view.

Linza stood up behind a tree, the blue eyes assuming a narrower shape. That tolerant face had gone almost dry of emotion. The lips were thin to the point of being bloodless, the lines running down from either corner lay deep as if slashed by a knife. Lifting his gun and holding the snout of it in his free palm a moment, he stared at the nearing fugitive. "I shall give him the chance he would have given me," he whispered, and stepped from the trees directly in front of Denton.

"Throw up your hands, Will!"

Denton's body seemed to spring up from the saddle, every muscle turning and twisting. The sun flashed in his eyes, the jerk of his head loosened his hat and it fell off to let a mane of sorrel hair shake loosely around his temples. Still in motion, his arm dropped, ripped the holstered gun upward and outward. Henry Linza raised his own weapon, took a cool aim at the chest broadly presented to him and fired once. Denton flinched back, sagged and fell from the saddle. There was no farewell; turning from the momentum of his fall, he stared sightlessly at the sky.

The man at the cabin let out a great cry. Linza wheeled to see him running forward in great stumbling strides and the sheriff's metal words sheared through the space. "Drop your gun right there!"

The man halted, cast his gun from him and came on, still cursing. Linza walked forward to the dead Will Denton and stared down. The outlaw's face, streaked with dirt and covered with a stubble beard, looked up with still a measure of that hot passion and that wild lawlessness that had been his at the moment of surprise. Linza's head fell lower and the figure of his one-time friend grew blurred.

"So there's the difference between his kind and mine," said Linza, trying to keep his voice clear. "He's dead — I'm alive."

The other man ran up, halted there. "He mistook the signal! I meant for him to keep away! I wasn't satisfied at all! I had a hunch something was wrong! But he got the signal twisted and come on in! Damn you, Linza!"

"No matter," grunted Linza. "Now or later — this is the end he was bound to meet. It was in the book. But it's hard to see him lyin' there."

"Yeah?" snarled the man. "Still yuh hounded him across the land and got him. It wasn't too hard to do that!"

Henry Linza's jaw came out to make him again seem as if he were biting into something. "You bet not. I will not lie and I won't dodge. Not for him or any other lawbreaker, even down to my own brother. And that goes as long as I carry this star. Go back there and get your horse. I am takin' him to Bonita for a Christian burial — as he would have done with me had he carried the star."

Ernest Haycox during his lifetime was considered the dean among authors of Western fiction. When the Western Writers of America was first organized in 1953, what became the Golden Spur Award for outstanding achievement in writing Western fiction was first going to be called the "Erny" in homage to Haycox. He was born in Portland, Oregon and, while still an undergraduate at the University of Oregon in Eugene, sold his first short story to the OVERLAND MONTHLY. His name soon became established in all the leading pulp magazines of the day, including Street and Smith's WESTERN STORY MAGAZINE and Doubleday's WEST MAGAZINE. His first novel, FREE GRASS, was published in book form in 1929. In 1931 he broke into the pages of COLLIER'S and from that time on was regularly featured in this magazine, either with a short story or a serial that was later published as a novel. In the 1940s his serials began appearing in THE SATURDAY EVENING POST and it was there that modern classics such as BUGLES IN THE AFTERNOON (1944) and CANYON PASSAGE (1945) were first published. Both of these novels were also made into major motion pictures although, perhaps, the film most loved and remembered is STAGECOACH (United Artists, 1939) directed by John Ford and starring John Wayne, based on Haycox's short story "Stage to Lordsburg." No history of the Western story in the 20th Century would be possible without reference to Haycox's fiction and his tremendous influence on other writers of stature, such as Peter Dawson, Norman A. Fox, Wayne D. Overholser, and Luke Short, among many. During his last years, before his premature death from abdominal carcinoma, he set himself the task of writing historical fiction which he felt would provide a fitting legacy and the consummation of his life's work. He almost always has an involving story to tell and one in which there is something not so readily definable that raises it above its time, an image possibly, a turn of phrase, or even a sensation, the smell of dust after rain or the solitude of an Arizona night. Haycox was an author whose Western fiction has made an abiding contribution to world literature.

We hope you have enjoyed this Large Print book. Other Thorndike Press or Chivers Press Large Print books are available at your library or directly from the publishers. For more information about current and upcoming titles, please call or write, without obligation, to:

Thorndike Press
P.O. Box 159
Thorndike, Maine 04986
USA
Tel. (800) 223-6121 (U.S. & Canada)
In Maine call collect: (207) 948-2962

OR

Chivers Press Limited
Windsor Bridge Road
Bath BA2 3AX
England
Tel. (0225) 335336

All our Large Print titles are designed for easy reading, and all our books are made to last.